The **OBJECT** OF HIS **AFFECTION**

MARCIA LYNN McCLURE

Published by Distractions Ink
1290 Mirador Loop N.E.
Rio Rancho, NM 87144

Published by Distractions Ink
©Copyright 2015 by M. Meyers
A.K.A. Marcia Lynn McClure
Cover Photography by ©Konradbak/Dreamstime.com
Cover Design and Interior Graphics by Sandy Ann
Allred/Timeless Allure

First Printed Edition: April 2015
All character names and personalities in this work of fiction are
entirely fictional, created solely in the imagination of the author.
Any resemblance to any person living or dead is coincidental.

McClure, Marcia Lynn, 1965—
*The Object of His Affection*: a novella/by Marcia Lynn McClure.

ISBN: 978-0-9861307-6-2
Library of Congress Control Number: 2015938870
Printed in the United States of America

**To my darling, dearest friend, Amy (Aimes)—**

*Why yes…at last we do! (Wink wink!)*

*Just for you.*

# CHAPTER ONE

It was cold—so miserably cold. Athena knew by the numbness in her own fingers and toes that Annabel's, Marta's, and Bronwen's must be frozen stiff. Yet she hoped that their merriment—in singing Christmas carols on the doorsteps or in the parlors of those who opened their doors or invited them inside for a moment—would offset their discomfort. After all, a happy heart warmed many a frigid soul, as well as ice-cold appendages.

As a child, Athena had adored caroling. It was with warm fondness that she thought back on all those Christmas seasons of the past when her entire family would carol to their neighbors. Always her mother had made puddings, cakes, and other sweet treats to bring with them, to give as gifts of affection to their kind townsfolk and friends. And once the caroling was at an end, the Monroe family—Athena's father, mother, and sisters Annabel, Marta, and Bronwen—would return to their own home to sit before the fire and enjoy roasted chestnuts and wassail.

But this Christmas season—the season that had always been bright and shining, the season that had always been to Athena a time to consider others, to give and serve—this Christmas season was stark in opposition!

Never had Athena imagined that she would find herself in such dire, desperate circumstances as she did then. As she followed her younger sisters to the next door on the row of lovely houses—houses so similar to the one in which she and her sisters had spent only the very last Christmas season—she hoped that the next kind family to open the door might offer her sisters (and herself as well) a token of goodwill—a warm mug of wassail, a small butter biscuit, anything for their stomachs. Even in that moment, Athena's stomach growled with being famished, and although she and Annabel could endure the extreme hunger better than Marta and

Bronwen, who were so much younger than they were, it was still a frightening pain and misery.

"I hope *someone* offers us a bowl of pudding...or at least a biscuit," Annabel whispered to Athena as they walked behind their little sisters. "Or at least offers something for the little girls."

"As do I," Athena said. "I've nothing at home but thin broth for supper tonight. Very thin broth."

Though the worry and disappointment shone plain in Annabel's eyes, she forced a smile and said, "Oh, it will be plenty, Athena. Perhaps it won't be old Heather's hearty beef stew, but we'll imagine that it is, eh? We'll close our eyes and pretend that Heather is still our cook and that our thin broth is truly one of Heather's beefy meals. It will be fine."

Athena choked back the tears threatening to spill from her eyes, nodded, and tried to smile.

Annabel put her arms around her older sister's shoulders. "All will be well, Athena," she said. "Aren't you the one always telling us so? Assuring us that God is with us, even as we struggle? That there are those who struggle far worse than we do?"

"And it's true," Athena said. "I suppose I'm just especially tired tonight. And being that it's nearly Christmas...and I'm so worried that I won't have enough wages to get some small thing for the girls from Father Christmas, and…"

"Take heart, Athena, my love," Annabel soothed. "Perhaps the very next door we carol to will find a kind family with a warm hearth they are wanting to share this evening. After all, Marta and Bronwen are the most darling of little girls, with their springing curls and pink cheeks. And we all of us have the loveliest singing voices! Everyone has always said we sound just like Christmas angels."

Athena's heart lightened a little. "You're right, Annabel, my darling," she said. "We do sound like Christmas angels. And goodness knows, it won't take much to satisfy Marta and Bronwen's small stomachs. Even just a bite of Christmas pudding would do. Then we can go home to our small but warm and cozy little Camden Town hovel, curl up in our little bed, and get some sleep. Tomorrow's another day, after all, isn't it? And God will care for us…always. We might not have the wealth, good food, and pretty finery we once had…but we have one another, yes?"

"Yes," Annabel agreed.

Marta and Bronwen began to run far ahead of their older sisters then—and right up onto the stoop of a warm-windowed row house with holly and pine adorning the outer door.

"This one, Athena!" Marta called in a loud whisper. "Hurry!"

Athena exchanged amused glances with Annabel as they swiftly hastened to join their little sisters on the stoop.

"You two need to quit lagging so far behind," Bronwen giggled. "It's growing late, and people will be retiring to their beds soon."

"Our apologies, Mistress Bronwen," Athena teased her rosy-cheeked and littlest sister. "Now…what shall we sing?"

"'God Rest Ye, Merry Gentlemen,'" Bronwen suggested.

"Oh, not again!" Marta whined, however.

"How about, 'Here We Come A-wassailing' then?" Bronwen countered.

"Yes!" Marta exclaimed. "I love 'Here We Come A-wassailing'! It makes me feel warm and comfortable inside."

"That's it then," Athena said, smiling at her little sisters. "You start us out, Annabel, please."

"I'd be honored," Annabel said. Clearing her throat, she began, *"Here we come a-wassailing among the leaves so green."*

With a smile of renewed hope and joy in the beauty of the season, Athena joined with her sisters, and the little girls leapt in with, *"Here we come a-wandering so fair to be seen. Love and joy come to you, and to you your wassail too, and God bless you and send you a happy new year. And God send you a happy new year."*

At just that very moment—just as Athena was beginning to accept the lot their father's unwise speculating had tossed them into, that his death had tossed them into—the door to the lovely, brightly lit, warm-windowed house opened.

Annabel, Marta, and Bronwen continued to sing, *"We are not daily beggars who go from door to door..."*

But Athena all but entirely lost her voice. Quickly she held her ragged muffler scarf up to her face—to hide her mouth, nose, and cheeks. For there, standing in the doorway of the welcoming domicile, stood Mrs. Florence Dandridge! Of all the doors in London, how had Marta and Bronwen managed to find this door, the door belonging to the Dandridge family?

"Oh, how perfectly charming!" Mrs. Dandridge exclaimed in a whisper as Athena and her sisters continued to sing. Being the kind, well-mannered woman that she was, Florence Dandridge waited until the song had finished before applauding and exclaiming further, "Oh, that was so lovely, girls! So very, very lovely!" Bending over and placing her hands on her knees, Mrs. Dandridge looked Marta and Bronwen directly in their eyes. Smiling, she pled, "Won't you come inside a moment and sing another song for me? I have wassail here in the parlor and a plate of Christmas biscuits to tempt you."

Athena gasped, for before she could reach out and stay the girls from going into the Dandridge home, Marta and Bronwen each curtsied, simultaneously said, "Yes, mum," and nearly dashed inside.

Only Annabel paused. "Athena? Isn't that Mrs...." she began.

"Yes," Athena confirmed in a whisper.

Mrs. Dandridge's attention was on Athena and Annabel then. "Oh, do come in, ladies. Let's all have another song or two and enjoy some merry sweets together."

Athena exchanged worried yet defeated glances with Annabel. There was nothing they could do now—not with Marta and Bronwen already in the house.

Awash with humiliation, Athena stepped forward and into the house. Annabel followed as Athena removed her scarf, forced a smile, and looked at Mrs. Dandridge, saying, "Happy Christmas, Mrs. Dandridge."

Athena thought she was prepared for the astonishment she knew would leap to Mrs. Dandridge's face—but she wasn't. As the woman's cheeks, which had been so lovely and pink only a moment before, drained of all color and as her smile faded and her eyes widened with something akin to— was it guilt?—Athena offered, "We did not mean to inconvenience you…not one whit, Mrs. Dandridge. The girls, they only wanted to go caroling this evening and—"

"Athena, my girl," Mrs. Dandridge exclaimed, however. "How…how wonderful to see you again! Oh, please do come in!"

"Thank you," Athena began. "But we really must be going. It's growing late and—"

"Oh, nonsense," Mrs. Dandridge kindly argued. "Come in and enjoy some wassail."

And then, as often is the case, just as one thinks matters cannot possibly get any more humiliating, Mrs. Dandridge called over her shoulder. "Rafe! Rafe, darling, come at once. We have carolers…and you'll never guess who is among them!"

As Athena thought she might drop dead of humiliation, Mrs. Dandridge hurried to where Marta and Bronwen were standing by the warm hearth watching the fire glow.

"Darlings," she said, taking Bronwen with one hand and Marta with the other, "see this little table here?" Mrs. Dandridge nodded toward a small table nearby, laden with a bowl of wassail and several plates of various biscuits. "You have your fill, girls! As many biscuits as you like and all the wassail you need to warm you up. All right?"

"Thank you, mum," Marta said.

"Yes, mum. Thank you!" Bronwen giggled as both girls hastened to the table.

Athena held her breath, watching her sisters in case they should forget their manners—but they didn't, and she breathed easier.

"What's all this, Mother?" a deep, very masculine voice resonated.

Athena gulped. Rafe Dandridge—the older of the Dandridge boys she'd grown up with. Fenton, the younger, had been her friend, of course—her very close friend. But Rafe Dandridge had always unnerved her. And as Athena slowly turned to look at him, she remembered why.

There he stood, with his tall, brooding persona, his severe countenance—and his heart-stirring good looks. Hair as dark as sable and eyes that flashed like rare bronze diamonds, Rafe Dandridge had always given Athena the sense that he could look into her soul—read her most secretive thoughts.

"You remember the Monroe girls, don't you, darling?" Mrs. Dandridge asked her son.

As Rafe Dandridge looked first to Marta and Bronwen, then to Annabel, and finally to Athena, she felt that, had there been any contents in her stomach, they would've presented themselves all over Mrs. Dandridge's floor.

"They've come caroling, Rafe darling," Mrs. Dandridge explained, "to wish us a happy Christmas."

But as Rafe continued to stare at Athena a moment, it was she that could read his thoughts—and she knew he was thinking they were little more than beggars, come to pitifully fill their bellies on his mother's kind offerings.

"Of course," he said then, however. "How good to see you all again." Striding directly toward Athena, he offered her his hand.

She paused a moment, considering which was worse: to take his hand with her threadbare, tattered mitten or to risk offending him with not accepting his hand.

Habit and a lifelong adherence to propriety won her over, however, and Athena indeed accepted Rafe Dandridge's handshake of welcome.

"Miss Athena," he said.

"Yes, sir," Athena assured him.

Rafe Dandridge did something infamously dangerous: he smiled. And Rafe Dandridge's smile was not one a woman could ignore—even had she wanted to—for it was hypnotic in quality and beguiled reciprocation from even the most hardhearted of old crones. Thus, Athena smiled at him, even for the fact she was more uncomfortable than ever she had been in the whole of her life.

"And this would be Miss Annabel," Rafe said then, nodding to Annabel and instantly inducing a smile from her as well.

Rafe then looked to where Marta and Bronwen stood politely nibbling on one biscuit each. Athena's heart panged for them, for she knew they would have loved nothing more than to gobble down every biscuit laid out on the table.

"And the little ones," Rafe commented. He glanced to his mother, and a look of understanding passed between them. "Well, they look to be growing up to rival the loveliness of their elder sisters, now don't they, Mother?"

"Indeed," Mrs. Dandridge agreed. She smiled at Athena then, and it was a smile of guilt as well as mercy. "Oh, do come sit for a moment, Athena, Annabel. Have a cup of wassail with us, won't you?"

"Oh, b-but we really...we really should get the girls home and tucked into bed," Athena stammered. "It's quite late, after all, and—"

"Please," Mrs. Dandridge said, taking Athena's hands in her own.

"Another quarter of an hour won't hurt, will it?" Annabel asked Athena.

Athena could see the desperation in Annabel's eyes—the soulful want of something sweet to eat and a warming drink.

"Please, Miss Monroe," Rafe interceded. "After all, you wouldn't deprive my mother of the merriment of sharing a few minutes of the season with old friends, would you?"

"Yes, please," Mrs. Dandridge pled once more. "Do stay, Athena. Just for a little while."

Glancing from Annabel's desperate expression to the beseeching ones of her little sisters, Athena at last nodded. "Very well. As long as it's not an imposition or—"

"It's not!" Mrs. Dandridge exclaimed with delight. "Now do take a seat, dears, and I'll ladle you each a cup of wassail."

"This way," Rafe said. Being the gentleman that he was, he placed his hand at the small of Athena's back as he gestured that she and Annabel should sit on a comfortable-looking sofa at hand. And for one instant—a brief, fleeting instant at that—his touch caused Athena to experience a sense of safety she had not felt in a long, very long time.

As she indeed took a seat on the Dandridges' comfortable sofa, Athena experienced a mingling of emotions—anger, envy, overwhelming sadness, fear, desperation. Oh, she held her countenance well enough—maintained an expression of strength and of being calm. But inside—inside she was silently crying out in anguish. What had happened to her mother and father was not at all the fault of Florence, Fenton, or Rafe Dandridge. Blame for the tragedy that had befallen the Monroe family was not even to be placed on Edgar Dandridge—Florence Dandridge's late husband, father to Rafe and Fenton.

Nevertheless, Athena could not help but feel anger, or at least frustration, as she sat in the near opulence of the Dandridge home. Especially when she and her sisters had once lived just as comfortably—and yet would be returning to their hovel that night to sleep all in the same bed, curled up together to keep warm, like church mice in a donations box.

"Well now," Mrs. Dandridge began as she carefully ladled out two cups of wassail. Turning and taking the cups to Athena and Annabel, she continued, "It is so very good to see you girls again."

Mrs. Dandridge offered the wassail to Athena and her sister. "And you as well, Mrs. Dandridge," Athena managed with a smile. She took a dainty sip of the warm wassail, so spicy with flavor. "And I see you still brew the best wassail in London," Athena added. For it was the truth.

Mrs. Dandridge smiled, sighing with satisfaction. "You always were the kindest young woman of my acquaintance, Athena. I'm…I'm so very glad that hasn't changed."

"And how are you faring this season?" Rafe inquired. "Are you enjoying the pleasantries of the holiday?"

"As much as can be expected in our circumstances," Annabel answered.

Athena glanced scoldingly at her sister and then herself answered, "We are enjoying the season, Mr. Dandridge. In fact, it is what finds us out and about on this frosty winter night—spreading our own happiness throughout the township by caroling."

"Yes!" Marta exclaimed. "We love caroling! And Athena says the brisk weather makes our noses as red as summer cherries. And we like our noses to be red, don't we, Bronwen?"

"We do," Bronwen agreed. Bronwen looked to Mrs. Dandridge then, saying, "Thank you so much, mum, for the wassail and biscuits. Your Christmas biscuits are quite the most delicious I've ever tasted!"

Mrs. Dandridge laughed, cupped Bronwen's sweet face in one elegant hand, and said, "Why, thank you, darling! You may have as many as you like."

"May we have as many as we like, Athena?" Marta asked.

Athena could see the hunger and desire in her little sisters' eyes. Yet propriety was of the utmost importance, and so she answered, "I think it would be best mannered to limit yourselves to two more biscuits each. After all, we must think of the other carolers who may visit the Dandridges, mustn't we?"

Marta and Bronwen both nodded. Then Marta, looking to Bronwen, said, "That makes proper sense, doesn't it? A bit like thinking of all the other children in the world that Father Christmas must visit on Christmas Eve, instead of asking him for everything we want for ourselves, don't you think?"

"Yes," Bronwen agreed. "Exactly so." Looking to Mrs. Dandridge then, the littlest Monroe sister smiled and said, "But thank you for offering to let us have our fill, Mrs. Dandridge. You are a very kind lady. I'm so glad we came caroling to your door!"

"Oh, you are little darlings, aren't you?" Mrs. Dandridge laughed.

Athena sipped her wassail as slowly as she could—even though she wanted to gulp it down to soothe the growling of her stomach—and watched as Mrs. Dandridge pulled a line to one of the house bells. The house bell chimed, and almost instantly a young man appeared.

"Yes, mum?" the young man greeted his mistress as he bowed.

"Charles," Mrs. Dandridge began, "would you be so kind as to fetch one of our gift tins? I so want the Monroe girls to enjoy their fill of Christmas biscuits tonight."

"Oh, that's not necessary, Mrs. Dandridge," Annabel began.

But Athena, as always, remembered her manners over her pride and said, "How kind, Mrs. Dandridge. I'm certain Marta and Bronwen would love nothing more than to fairly gorge on Christmas biscuits for breakfast tomorrow. Isn't that right, girls?"

Giggling, Marta and Bronwen nodded in unison as Bronwen admitted, "Indeed we would!"

"Then you shall!" Mrs. Dandridge laughed. "Thank you, Charles," she added, letting the young house servant know that he should go ahead and fetch a gift tin.

"Yes, mum," Charles said, offering another bow.

Athena watched as Charles began to leave the room on his errand. Rafe Dandridge took hold of his arm, however, lowering his voice and telling the young man something she could not hear.

"Of course, sir," Charles said, nodding to Rafe. Charles left the room then, and Rafe offered a friendly grin and nod when Athena's gaze lingered on him with curiosity and suspicion for a moment.

"Oh!" Mrs. Dandridge exclaimed then. "I swear I'm as scattered as leaves in the wind!" Choosing a plate of biscuits from the small table, the lovely woman hurried to where Athena and Annabel sat. "I quite forgot to offer you young ladies a Christmas biscuit, as well."

"Thank you, Mrs. Dandridge," Athena said, choosing a delicious-looking biscuit for herself. "I am overwhelmed at being so spoiled."

Annabel chose a biscuit as well, saying, "Yes! I wasn't aware that caroling could be quite so scrumptious!"

Everyone smiled and laughed a little as a courtesy in lieu of the obvious awkwardness in the room.

Athena looked up then to see Rafe Dandridge studying her through narrowed, rather suspicious-looking eyes. Again his unrivaled handsomeness unnerved her greatly, and a sudden feeling of being frantic for escape washed over her. Glancing around, she saw that both she and Annabel had drained their wassail cups and finished their biscuits. The younger girls were finished as well and now stood gazing wistfully at the remaining delicacies on Mrs. Dandridge's china plates.

"Well, girls, we best be on our way," Athena said, rising to her feet. "We've several more houses to carol to before it's too late. And it's quite a bit of a walk home as well."

"Oh, must you go so soon?" Mrs. Dandridge asked. Athena thought that the woman looked truly sincere in her desire for them to linger.

"I'm afraid we must," Athena answered, however. "The girls do need their rest."

Charles arrived then, handing a basket to Mrs. Dandridge. "Mr. Rafe suggested a basket might serve better, mum."

As Rafe and his mother exchanged glances of understanding, Athena felt a blush of humiliation rise to her cheeks. The basket was obviously heaping with good things to eat—far more than merely a tin of biscuits.

But as Athena's pride readied to refuse the gift of charity, it was Rafe who spoke. "I wanted to be certain the little ones get their fill of Mother's biscuits for their breakfast. And after all...our families are nearly lifelong acquaintances."

"Bravo, Rafe! I'm so glad you had your wits about you, for obviously mine were numbed," Mrs. Dandridge exclaimed as she rather pushed the basket into Annabel's arms.

"We'll be on our way then," Athena said. She forced a smile and, looking from Mrs. Dandridge to Rafe and back, added, "Thank you again for having us in. It was wonderful to see you both once more."

"Oh, darling Athena," Mrs. Dandridge whispered as she unexpectedly reached out and embraced Athena. "Thank you for blessing us with your company. You're all such lovely young ladies. I'm so very glad to know you're all well."

"Thank you," Athena said, halfheartedly returning the woman's embrace. "Happy Christmas!"

"Happy Christmas," Mrs. Dandridge said, releasing Athena.

Athena was moved by the moisture brimming in Mrs. Dandridge's eyes then. Her humility, as well as her guilt and sadness at the plight of Athena and her sisters, was obvious in her countenance, and it warmed Athena's heart toward the woman.

"Happy Christmas," Annabel said, offering a curtsy.

"Happy Christmas," chimed Marta and Bronwen.

"And thank you again for letting us gorge on your biscuits, ma'am," Marta added.

Mrs. Dandridge smiled, saying, "You're so very welcome, darling."

"Are you certain you wouldn't rather I called up the carriage to take you and your sisters home, Miss Monroe?" Rafe asked.

Looking up into his brooding yet mesmerizing expression, Athena assured him, "I'm certain," even though she would have relished a warm, quick carriage ride home. "We are caroling, after all."

"As you wish," Rafe said. Then—again causing an overwhelming sensation of yearning to feel safe and cared for, protected once more—Rafe Dandridge placed a strong hand at the small of Athena's back as he escorted her toward the door.

"Thank you again for caroling at our door, girls," Mrs. Dandridge said.

"You're welcome. It was our pleasure," Athena said as she saw the woman brush tears from her cheeks.

Athena was touched by Mrs. Dandridge's obvious emotion, and it softened her heart. Though the lot of her sisters and herself was undeniably a miserable one, it truly was no fault of Mrs. Dandridge or her sons, and she felt sympathy for Mrs. Dandridge's needless guilt.

"Good night, Miss Athena," Rafe said as he opened the door. He nodded to each of Athena's sisters in turn, and soon they were once more standing on the stoop of the Dandridge home.

Frost was falling through the cold night air, and little Bronwen said, "Oh, how lovely! Don't you think, Athena? It looks just like diamonds are sifting down through the night, doesn't it?"

Athena smiled at her little sister and said, "Yes, darling...it does."

"Now I'm more cold than even I was before," Annabel grumbled. She frowned at Athena a moment, adding, "And there you were, Athena, trying to alleviate that woman of any guilt and hard feelings she might have where we are concerned—when her husband is the very reason for our destitute state of being!"

"Our state is not Mr. Dandridge's fault," Athena said. "And it certainly isn't Mrs. Dandridge's fault. Father made his own decisions, and he made them in thinking he was doing what would be best for our futures." She smiled at Annabel and gently caressed first Bronwen's cheek and then Marta's. "And we have each other, still, don't we? We have a home and a lovely Christmas tree awaiting our attention when we return. So chins up, my sweets. It's nearly Christmas!"

Bronwen smiled up at her oldest sister. "Now may we sing 'God Rest Ye, Merry Gentlemen,' Athena? Please? It will keep us warm as we walk. I'm certain of it!"

Athena smiled, even laughed. "Of course, Brony. 'God Rest Ye, Merry Gentlemen' it is."

Athena took hold of Annabel's mittened hand, squeezing it with reassurance. "We have each other, Annabel, and that's more than a lot of people have."

Annabel nodded—smiled.

Bronwen began, "*God rest ye, merry gentlemen, let nothing you dismay…*"

And Athena's heart was warmed by remembrance of the season and what it existed for. *"Remember Christ, our Savior, was born on Christmas day,"* she joined.

Marta and Annabel united in singing the carol then too. And as the Monroe sisters walked toward home, singing carols of the season to warm their hearts, Athena thought, *At least we're alive,* and determined that her faith in the New Year finding them all in a better lot would not go unnoticed by the Son of God, whose birth they celebrated with their beloved carols.

# CHAPTER TWO

"I feel positively ill, Rafe," Florence Dandridge said as she gazed out the window into the cold winter's night. "They're destitute! So obviously destitute, so thin, wearing hardly more than rags." Collapsing onto the sofa in the parlor, Florence smoothed a dark strand of her hair from her temple and brushed tears from her cheeks. "If your father were still alive...I think I'd hate him for it."

"Mr. Monroe made his own choices, Mother," Rafe grumbled. Yet as his frown deepened, he added, "But I cannot abide that it was Father who led him to it—to ruination and death...and the abandonment of his children."

"We have to do something for the Monroe girls, Rafe. We must!" Florence insisted. Straightening her posture, she added, "It is clear they are living in the city. At least we know that they are alive and somewhere near...Camden Town, perhaps. We must find where they are living and do something to help them, Rafe."

"Agreed," Rafe said. "That is why I have sent Charles to follow them home tonight...so that we may discover where their residence is and its condition."

Florence smiled up at her eldest son. "I should've known you already had something in mind, darling."

Standing once more, Florence retrieved a plate of Christmas biscuits from the small parlor table, rather plopped back down onto the sofa, and, setting the plate on her lap with the evident intention of eating her fill of the sweet things, exhaled a heavy sigh. "The girls were so well-mannered, even for the fact it was sorely apparent they were near to starving." She wiped more tears from her cheeks.

Rafe watched his mother shove an entire biscuit into her mouth and begin munching.

"What can be done, do you think?" his mother asked him. "If Athena is anything close to the independent-minded lady her mother was, it will not be an easy task, attempting to convince her to allow us to help them."

"We'll manage it, Mother," Rafe assured her. "One way or the other, I will not allow the Monroe daughters to linger in misery. I owe them that, in the very least."

"You owe them?" Florence questioned, however. "It wasn't you who sent their father to ruin, Rafe." Shoving another biscuit into her mouth, she added, "It was your father's fault...not yours."

Rafe shrugged. "I am my father's eldest son, and because I am who I am, any misery endured now by the Monroe children by way of my sire...well, it falls to me to do what I can to right Father's wrongs where they are concerned." He paused, exhaled a heavy sigh, and added, "The name of Dandridge...it has been blackened by Father's ill deeds, and now also by Fenton's reckless behavior. Therefore, if our name is ever to inspire thoughts of honor among good people again, it is up to me to make it so."

Frowning, Florence asked, "You want to help the Monroe girls simply to sweeten the taste of the name of Dandridge on human tongues again?"

Rafe smiled at his mother, knowing exactly what she was thinking. "Of course not, Mother. I want to help them. First and foremost, I want the Monroe girls to be warm, cared for…their futures secured."

As his mother smiled with approval and popped another biscuit into her mouth, Rafe continued, "But they were wronged by my father, and I will not excuse it. And that makes me responsible for their plight. Therefore, that is reason too for me to see to their well-being. Don't you agree?"

"Yes," Florence admitted. "I do understand you, Rafe…and I feel the same."

"Good," Rafe said, taking a seat next to his mother on the sofa. "Then we will wait for Charles's return and hear what he has to report." Rafe took a biscuit from the plate on his mother's lap, putting it whole into his mouth. "And then I will take action, Mother. I'm determined that the Monroe girls will never spend another day in hunger or cold."

"And they had wood burning in their hearth, Athena!" Marta exclaimed. "Wood, not coal. Oh, I've never smelled anything so wonderful as that wood burning."

Athena nodded in agreement. Smiling at the remembered fragrance of the burning wood in the Dandridge's hearth, she said, "Yes. I didn't realize how much I'd missed the aroma of wood burning. Coal…well, it's just not as soothing, is it?"

"Well, if Mr. Dandridge hadn't coaxed our father into speculation, we might have wood burning in our hearth, and our house might be as big and warm and lovely as theirs," Annabel grumbled.

Athena sighed with frustration. As she had told her sister many, many times before, she reminded again, "Father made his own decisions, Annabel. Mr. Dandridge cannot be blamed for the choices Father made."

"Why not?" Annabel asked as her temper rose. "Mr. Dandridge told Father all about the opportunity in speculation…and then turned on his heel and did not take the opportunity for himself. And the outcome? Well, you know it as well as I do. Mr. Dandridge retained his fortune, and our father lost his. Thus we live in poverty, and Mr. Dandridge's family lives in luxury."

"Father made his own choice, Annabel," Athena reminded her sister for the hundredth time. "You know as well as I do, for you were listening at the top of the stairs with me the day that Mr. Dandridge came to tell Father he had decided not to involve his money in the speculation venture." She paused, staring at her sister with love and understanding yet also reprimand in her gaze. "Father chose to speculate, and Mr. Dandridge chose not to. That is that."

"And besides, Annabel," Bronwen ventured, "can't you simply be glad that we had ham and warm bread for supper tonight, instead of thin broth alone? And that was because Mrs. Dandridge gave us the basket. Can't you be glad for that tonight?"

"Yes," Marta agreed. "It's only two days 'til Christmas, Annabel. Please, let's enjoy what we do have and not nest so much on what we've lost."

Athena smiled at Marta and Bronwen, kissed them each on one cheek, and then looked to Annabel and said, "Out of the mouth of babes…"

"Oft comes porridge," Annabel finished, still scowling.

Yet as Athena laughed, amused by Annabel's changing the cliché she'd begun to more readily present humor than a lesson in wisdom, Annabel smiled as well.

Marta and Bronwen began to giggle as Marta said, "I see! Because babies often spit out their porridge if they're cross and not wanting to eat. That's very amusing, Annabel! Bravo!"

Bronwen threw her little arms around Annabel's neck, kissing her elder sister's cheek. "You see, Annabel?" the young girl said. "It is a happy time of year. A time for remembering the Christ child…his birth and sacrifice. We may be hungry sometimes, but at least we've not been nailed to a cross and had to bear the sins of all humanity."

"And we have ham and warm bread—and the largest tin of Christmas biscuits I've ever seen—all for us to enjoy," Marta added.

Athena smiled, awed by the resilience of her two youngest sisters. At times, she wondered if Marta and Bronwen were angels or some other cherubic hosts of heaven, come to comfort Annabel and herself when despair was near to devouring them completely. They were happy, no matter their circumstances.

And yet the pondering of Marta and Bronwen's youthful innocence and happiness caused dark thoughts to intrude on Athena's mind then. Perhaps her littlest sisters were happy now, but what would become of them if their circumstances remained unchanged? There was no hope in their futures, no hope of security and comfort, not when they were penniless—destitute. No doubt they would be forced to find employment before they reached the age of ten. And—God forbid, as Athena prayed—if something should happen to Athena before they were old enough to make their own way, they most certainly would be thrown into workhouses, to waste away in darkness and misery.

As the weathered old clock on the mantel struck eight, Athena forced her thoughts to the morrow.

"Come now, ladies," she said. "Morning will be here far too soon, so let's curl up in bed and dream about pretty things, shall we?"

"I'm going to dream about fairies," Bronwen said. She popped one more of Mrs. Dandridge's biscuits into her mouth and slid down from her chair.

"I'm going to dream about dollies and the smell of woodsmoke," Marta said.

"I'm going to dream that a handsome prince rides up to our hovel and carries me away to his palace," Annabel sighed wistfully—though she smiled as she took Marta's and Bronwen's hands and began leading them to the bed that they all shared in the corner of the room.

"And I'm going to dream that Mr. Eads will give me an extra shilling with my wages tomorrow," Athena said. "Then we can buy a Christmas pudding to go with our ham and biscuits."

Looking back over her shoulder to Athena, Annabel winked and said, "That *is* dreaming."

Once the four of them were tucked in as warmly as they could be for the night, Athena began her silent prayers. As always, she thanked God for every blessing he had showered down upon them— continued life and good health, her employment in Mr. Eads's kitchen, and the like. And when she'd thanked the Maker for all else her weary mind could think of, she humbly thanked him for leading Marta and Bronwen to the Dandridges' door. For it was thanks to God and the Dandridges that her sisters had fallen asleep without their bellies growling with hunger, for the first time in months.

Athena felt unworthy to ask God for anything at all, being that she knew he had already blessed them far more than some others enjoyed. Yet she knew the seriousness of their situation. And therefore, she asked for only one thing—though she knew God or His Son would be performing one of their miracles in order to grant what she was asking for. Athena asked for deliverance—that somehow she would be able to provide for her sisters far better than she provided now. That somehow their living conditions would be improved and that, somehow, she would be able to afford better food with which to nourish them.

And as the coal in the hearth glowed low with the intent of burning out, Athena drifted to sleep with Bronwen in her arms and Annabel and Marta at her back. For a moment, just before unconsciousness overtook her, she thought she smelled woodsmoke—thought she sensed the sweet aroma of Christmas biscuits baking in an oven—thought she again tasted the soothing spice of wassail as children's voices caroled somewhere in the distance.

# CHAPTER THREE

The floor was so cold! To Athena, it felt as if she were treading on ice as she hurried to the door to answer the knocking.

"But who can it possibly be at this hour?" Annabel asked as she set about preparing breakfast. "The sun hasn't even begun to rise!"

"Please speak softly, Annabel," Athena begged her sister. "The girls are still sleeping, and they need their rest."

Fetching her shawl from the hat rack near the front door, Athena turned the lock with trepidation. She too wondered who would be out and knocking on their door at such an early hour. She had thought quite seriously of ignoring the insistent pounding but decided to see who was there, in case it was a neighbor in need.

As Athena lifted the latch and pulled the door open a crack, however, she gasped in astonishment. There before her stood none other than Rafe Dandridge, and she thought that she would have been no more surprised had it been the prime minister himself come calling!

"M-Mr. Dandridge?" Athena stammered.

"Good morning, Miss Monroe," Rafe greeted, removing his hat and bowing a little. "I apologize for calling at such an inconvenient time. But I thought that you might have somewhere to be this morning any later—an errand or...or an employer to satisfy."

"Y-yes, I do," Athena confirmed. She swung the door fully open and said, "Please, do come in. It's terribly cold this morning...though I'm not sure it's any warmer in here. But at least the wind and fog won't get to you."

"Thank you," Rafe said, stepping inside.

At once, Athena noticed that he was so tall that he could not stand his full height while in their little hovel. Thus, she offered, "Please sit down," as she indicated a chair at their table. "I-I have to admit that I'm quite taken aback at having opened the door to find you standing on the other side, Mr. Dandridge," Athena admitted. "Oh, may we get you anything? Water? Tea?"

Annabel cleared her throat, her eyes widening as Athena looked to her. Athena knew that Annabel was concerned in knowing that Athena had offered tea to Mr. Dandridge, when she well knew they had none to give him.

But Athena knew Rafe would politely decline. He was quite astute, after all, and Athena knew he would accept nothing from them—for he knew they had nothing to give.

"No, but thank you," he answered.

Athena heard Annabel sigh with relief.

"How may we help you, Mr. Dandridge?" Athena asked. She knew he had come for a purpose. A prosperous, handsome, successful man like Rafe Dandridge did not simply stop in at a hovel in Camden Town to visit with old acquaintances.

Rafe looked to Annabel a moment and then to Athena. "May I speak with you privately for a moment, Miss Monroe?"

Something akin to anxiety blended with curiosity welled inside Athena's bosom. "Of course." She looked Annabel, who simply nodded and strode to the furthest corner of the room, sat down, and picked up her darning. Athena knew that Annabel would hear every word that passed between Rafe and herself, but it was the best that could be done in the promise of more privacy.

"I'll be plain, Miss Monroe," Rafe began when Athena looked back to him.

"Yes?" she urged. Her nerves were quite in knots! He was an intimidating presence, and she could not imagine what his reasons were for calling.

"My father led yours into financial ruination," he began.

"Oh…oh no, no. What is past is past, and my father made his own decisions," Athena began to babble.

"Please, Miss Monroe," Rafe said, his voice low and commanding yet polite. "Please hear all I have come to say to you."

Athena blushed under his piercing gaze and nodded. "Yes…yes, of course," she said. "Forgive me."

Rafe continued, "My father led yours into ruination. At least, that is the way my mother and I feel. My mother believes your mother died of a broken heart. And her death was followed shortly by your father's…who, I am to understand, took his own life."

"Yes," Athena whispered. Pain gripped her heart then—pain in loss, pain in heartbreak, pain in the misery that had befallen her sisters and herself.

"I won't mince words or waste your valuable time any further, Miss Monroe," Rafe persisted. "Facts are facts. And would it be a fair assessment to say that your circumstances are less than comfortable? That your future and your sisters' are in question?"

Though her face blushed crimson with humiliation, Athena straightened her posture and admitted, "Yes."

"Then I have come to offer you a…shall we say, a contract," he said.

"A contract?" Athena asked.

"Yes…of sorts," Rafe answered.

Athena looked away a moment as shame began to consume her. Rafe had come to offer charitable contributions to her, and his guilt over what he perceived as a wrong his father had done was his reasoning.

"You've come to offer us money then? Charity?" she asked.

"No," Rafe answered. Athena looked back to him then as he said, "I've come to offer a contract to you, one that will benefit your sisters—see them warm, safe, cared for, and with great hopes in their futures—but at a great cost to you...your personal sacrifice."

Athena frowned. She wanted nothing more than to see her sisters safe, fed, warm, comfortable, and with actual hope in the future. Yet a great trepidation began to wash over her.

Still, for the sake of her sisters, she asked, "What great cost to me? What sacrifice?" She shook her head a moment, even giggled a little, adding, "What could be any worse than how we are existing now? How I am existing?"

"Marriage to me," Rafe plainly stated.

"What did you say?" Athena gasped, suddenly breathless with astonishment.

Looking directly into her eyes, Rafe leaned forward in his chair, somewhat lowering his voice as he spoke, "I am asking you to marry me...so that I may provide for you and your sisters all that you need, and much of what you may want."

Seeming to recognize that Athena was still too stunned to speak, Rafe continued. "If you agree to marry me, I will take you and your sisters from here on the morrow. You will come to live with my mother and myself, and we will be married the day after tomorrow."

"Married? On Christmas Day?" Athena breathed.

"Yes," Rafe affirmed. "Thereafter you and I will decide what is best for your sisters…such as, does your sister Annabel wish to attend finishing school? What school do you wish your little sisters to attend? The likes of those decisions will be made to benefit them as you wish. All of you will live comfortably, of course, and I will provide handsome dowries for each of your sisters so that they may marry well and remain comfortable throughout their lives." Rafe sat back in his chair. "Do you accept my contract of marriage?"

Athena was unable to speak at first, being so overwhelmed by Rafe's revealed plan. When she could speak, she asked, "And you would do all this, simply because you feel your father wronged mine…and thereby my sisters and me?"

"Pardon me, Miss Monroe," Rafe said as his eyes narrowed. "But there is nothing simple about this. And yes, I do feel responsible for you and your sisters because of my father's ill deeds. But do not mistake me. There is benefit for me as well in this."

"There is?" Athena asked. "I'm sorry, Mr. Dandridge, but I am witless, for I see no benefit for you in this—only heavy responsibility and a lifelong sentence of paying for what you feel your father has done ill."

Rafe inhaled a deep breath, exhaling it slowly before speaking again. "As you may or may not know, Miss Monroe, I am a man of business, and my schedule is stretched with commitments that must be met in order to maintain the health of my business." Rafe shifted in his chair, continuing, "I am not like my brother...whom you know very well, if I remember correctly."

Athena blushed, for she remembered the moment, years before, when Rafe entered the parlor a moment before his brother, Fenton, would have stolen a kiss from her.

"Where Fenton loves all things trivial and avoids responsibility and hard work as if they were a plague, I work hard to provide for my mother and myself," Rafe explained. "I am not professing to be a good man, but I am a hard worker. I am also opposite Fenton when it comes to pursuing women—courting, if you want to call it that. I have not the time nor patience to properly romance a woman...to find a woman suitable to be my wife. Yet I do want to leave a legacy, one far different than my father left to me. I do want to have children one day and to leave them in good care and healthy finances when my time on this earth is finished. I want to restore honor to the name of Dandridge and have that honor carried on." He paused, his eyes narrowing as he studied Athena for a moment. "Do you understand me?"

Athena nodded, even though the depth of what Rafe was saying was still sinking into her mind. Rafe Dandridge was offering to marry her. Marry her! Marry her and take care of her family—indeed take care of her for the rest of her life. Rafe would rescue Athena and her sisters from the misery they were mired in, and all he asked in return was that she provide him with children to leave his own legacy to.

Naturally, Athena knew to some extent what she must do to bear Rafe's children, and although that frightened her—or in the least, greatly unnerved her—the thought of having babies of her own, and of them being perhaps as attractive as Rafe Dandridge, appealed to her. All at once Athena began to realize that, as self-sacrificing as it may appear to Rafe should she accept his contract, it was, in truth, the very miracle she'd been praying for. Rafe Dandridge had arrived as an answer to her prayers! And no matter what Athena's personal sacrifice might be in accepting his proposal, she was humble in knowing that one did not refuse a gift from heaven.

Therefore, she answered Rafe, "I do understand. You will sacrifice your freedom of choice in a wife, in order to right the wrong you feel your father did to my family. You will provide everything my sisters and I stand in need of…and beyond need. And in return, you ask only that I marry you and provide children that you may leave a legacy for…a legacy they can be proud of."

"Yes, exactly," Rafe confirmed. "I know you will ask for time to consider what I have presented to you. Perhaps you wish to counsel with your sisters. But I would hope—"

"I don't need any more time to consider it, Mr. Dandridge," Athena interrupted. "I would be a fool to refuse such an offer from such a man as you." She laughed a little, still trying to gather it all in. "Do you truly think I would so value my own freedom to choose whom to marry, even if the opportunity did present itself…which I am doubtful it would? Do you really think I would put off such a gift as you have offered us?"

Rafe shrugged. "Considering that you will live out the rest of your life as wife to a man you hardly know…yes."

"Well, I will know you better by and by, won't I?" she asked, smiling at him.

Rafe nodded. "A rather uncomfortable thought to me, in truth," he mumbled. He paused a moment and then looked at her through narrowed, somewhat smoldering eyes and asked, "And what of my brother? What of Fenton? Will it be too difficult for you to be my wife, when it was he you were, shall we say, infatuated with, before hard times fell upon you?"

Athena blushed, offended and mortified by his inference. "If you mean to ask do you need to worry that I will practice some sort of infidelity—"

"No, no, no," Rafe interrupted, reaching out to place a reassuring hand on hers.

His hand was warm, even for his leather glove, and she could feel the strength in him just by the way his hand pressed over hers.

"I did not mean that. And I did not mean to offend you, Miss Monroe," he began to explain. "I simply wanted to make certain that it would not be too uncomfortable a situation for you to be in social contact with Fenton."

"No. It will not be uncomfortable for me," Athena stated. She was still mildly miffed at Rafe's inference, but she would not wreck a blessing of such profound magnitude simply because her pride had been pinched.

"Then, if you accept my offer—my contract—I will have the carriage come round for you and your sisters, and any belongings you may wish to bring, at sunrise tomorrow morning," Rafe said. "I think your sisters will enjoy spending Christmas Eve with my mother and her Christmas biscuits, don't you?"

Athena's heart softened once more, and she smiled at him. "Yes. I think they would," she admitted.

"Then do you accept my proposal, Miss Monroe?" he asked, staring at her as if she were a piece of mutton and he were a wolf.

His attractiveness was wildly unsettling, but Athena managed to maintain her straight posture, look him in the eye, and answer, "I do."

Rafe exhaled a sigh of relief, smiled, and nodded to her. "Thank you, Miss Monroe." He stood then, making ready to take his leave. "The carriage will arrive just after sunrise tomorrow then. And would it be all right…I mean, Mother wanted me to ask this…and I don't want to offend you again…"

"Then ask," Athena urged him. After all, how much lower could a woman get than to be living destitute in a hovel and having to marry a man simply to survive?

"Would it be all right if Mother's dressmaker and cobbler visited here this afternoon?" he ventured. "Mother would like to have new fittings completed for you and all your sisters at the earliest."

Athena inhaled a deep breath, surprised to find that she had more pride lingering within her than she thought.

"Again, Miss Monroe," Rafe began, "it is no less than she would do for her own children. I beg you to allow her this favor from you."

Closing her eyes a moment—unwilling to take anything more from Rafe Dandridge and his mother, yet knowing that in accepting his proposal, more would inevitably come—Athena nodded. "Very well," she managed.

"Please do not resent my mother's wanting to primp you all up like she would have her own daughters, had she had any," Rafe said in a lowered voice. "She thrives on doing for others…giving."

Athena nodded, her pride still pricked, but with understanding that her life was about to change.

"Fine then," Rafe said, smiling at her. "The carriage will call on the morrow, and Mother's dressmaker and cobbler will come today." He quirked one eyebrow, asking, "You will be at home when Mother's people come, won't you?"

"Y-yes, of course," Athena stammered as sudden realization overcame her. "I-I suppose I should inform Mr. Eads that I will no longer be working for him. Yes?"

"At once, yes," Rafe agreed.

As fear and doubt began to creep into every nook and cranny of Athena's being then, she looked up into Rafe's handsome face and asked, "The carriage will come tomorrow, yes? If…if I tell Mr. Eads I no longer need my position…he will not hire me again, if…if…"

Rafe reached out, taking Athena's hands in his own. "It will come, I promise," he told her. "And hopefully, if you remember anything at all about me from years past, you remember that my word is as solid and true as granite."

Athena nodded, even as the warmth from Rafe's gloved hands traveled up her arms to her shoulders. Smiling a little, she said, "I do remember that about you. And so I will trust in your word...and know that your carriage will arrive tomorrow morning."

"Good," Rafe said. Striding toward the door then, he opened it, making ready to take his leave.

"I-I haven't thanked you, Mr. Dandridge," Athena stammered as she followed him to the door.

He turned, looking down at her a moment. "You've accepted my offer, Miss Monroe," he said. "Furthermore, it is I who should be thanking you. Good day."

Rafe was gone then, and Athena stood staring at the door he'd closed behind him.

"Is it true, Athena?" Annabel asked in a whisper as she raced to her sister's side. "Are we to be saved? Are we truly to be saved from this miserable destitution?"

"It would seem so," Athena answered. "Though I am still not able to comprehend it fully." She turned to face Annabel, asking, "You did see Rafe Dandridge here in our hovel, didn't you? You did hear him offer to marry me, that we all should be freed from our pitiful plight, did you not?"

Annabel smiled, nodded, and assured her sister, "I did! Oh, I gloriously did, Athena!"

"Then...then I suppose it's true," Athena breathed. "Though I still cannot fathom that my prayers were answered so easily...and by means of Rafe Dandridge."

But Annabel giggled. "Oh, do believe it, Athena! After all, it was you who said God had not forsaken us, that he would send help...deliverance even. You just never mentioned that the help and deliverer he would send would be so handsome and rich!"

Suddenly Athena's head felt as if it were spinning, and in her dizziness, she muttered, "I...I suppose I should dress and...and inform Mr. Eads that I will no longer be working for him."

"No," Annabel said, taking her sister's hands in her own as she smiled with resplendence. "Let me go to Mr. Eads. You stay here and wake Marta and Bronwen. You feed them a good breakfast of ham and biscuits and tell them what has happened. It's your blessing to share, Athena." Annabel frowned then, adding, "And besides, it will give me great pleasure to tell that letch Mr. Eads that you are no longer beholden to him for wages. Great pleasure indeed."

Annabel's exuberance at the idea of being able to deliver the news to Mr. Eads brought a smile back to Athena's face. "All right, Annabel darling," she agreed. "You may go to Mr. Eads, and I will wake the little ones. It's one of my favorite moments of the day—waking them and watching them rub the sleep from their bright eyes. So go, and I will have breakfast waiting when you return."

Annabel nodded, giggled with excitement, and said, "I'll dress then." Her face was radiant as she added, "Oh, blessed day is this, Athena! We are saved!"

"Yes," Athena said as she watched Annabel dash off to ready for her errand. "So it would seem."

But as Athena went about preparing breakfast, she could not push visions of Rafe Dandridge from her mind. His wife? She was to marry Rafe Dandridge? Not Fenton, but Rafe? It was nearly inconceivable to her—to think that Marta and Bronwen's choice of a door to carol at had led to Athena's agreeing to marry a man she knew so very little about. Yet it was and always had been true that the Lord works in mysterious ways—and Athena could think of no more mysterious a thing than that.

# CHAPTER FOUR

"Happy Christmas, miss," the coachman greeted as he held Athena's hand, assisting her to step up into the carriage.

"Thank you, sir," Athena responded with a smile. "And a happy Christmas to you and yours."

"Why, thank you, miss," the jolly, round-bellied coachman chuckled as he closed the carriage door.

"I feel like a princess!" Marta whispered to Athena as she sat in her seat across from her older sisters. "This carriage...it's so grand!"

"It is very beautiful, isn't it?" Athena said, smiling at her little sister.

"And are we really going to live with the nice Christmas biscuit lady, Athena?" Bronwen asked.

"Of course we are," Annabel answered with mild impatience. "That's the hundredth time you've asked, Bronwen. Do you think we'd be in this carriage if we weren't going to live there?"

Bronwen hung her head and mumbled, "I'm sorry, Annabel. I just don't understand how it came to be, that's all."

Reaching across the carriage to take Bronwen's hand with reassurance, Athena said, "We need help, Bronwen, and Mr. Dandridge came to help us. I explained to you that I've known Mrs. Dandridge and her family since I was younger than you, remember?"

"Yes," Bronwen admitted. "But how is that I didn't know you loved him and wanted to marry him, Athena?"

Athena forced a smile. "Well, you'll understand when you're older. All right?"

Bronwen nodded, but Athena could see the child was still confused—and a bit frightened.

"And what a nice dress Mrs. Dandridge sent for you, yes?" Athena asked, redirecting Bronwen's attention. "Do you like your new dress, darling? Blue silk and blue velvet ribbon?"

Bronwen's expression brightened as she exclaimed, "Oh yes! It's the most beautiful dress I've ever seen, Athena!"

"And I like our new shoes," Marta added. "I'll have to teach you to properly use a button hook now, Bronwen."

"Yes, Marta, you will!" Bronwen giggled.

Athena looked to Annabel, and the two exchanged smiles.

"It does feel so…so different…being well dressed again," Annabel said. "I'd forgotten."

"Yes, it does," Athena admitted. She looked from Annabel and her lovely green dress to Marta and her soft pink one.

"And I love your dress, Athena!" Marta exclaimed. "You look so regal in that chestnut gown with just the tops of your shoulders showing."

Athena self-consciously tugged at the bodice of her dress a bit beneath her fur wrap. She'd never in all her life owned such a glamorous gown, and definitely not one that exposed so much of her shoulders.

"It's Christmas Eve," Athena began to explain. "Most people dress for Christmas Eve as if they were going to a ball. So Mrs. Dandridge chose dresses for us that were as near to ball gowns as she could find, being that her dressmaker had to choose from what she had already on hand in her shop." She smiled at her sisters then—all three of them. "I'm sure we'll have a lovely Christmas Eve with Mrs. Dandridge," she told them.

"And her son," Annabel added, "your soon-to-be husband."

"Yes…yes, of course," Athena said, forcing a smile.

The truth of it was that in the desperate early morning of the day before, Rafe Dandridge and his offer of a marriage of convenience had seemed plain to be a blessing from God above—an answer to Athena's prayers. Yet as the day had worn on—as Annabel had returned from informing Mr. Eads of Athena's leaving his employ, as the dressmaker and cobbler had arrived to take measurements, and as night had fallen—Athena's courage and determination to do whatever she must for the sake of her sisters' welfare had begun to tremble—and then to quake! She began to doubt that she could follow through with the plan, that she could marry Rafe Dandridge, that she could ever find the courage to bear children for him—even for her sisters' sakes.

Yet somehow Athena had managed to carry on. And when the dressmaker's boy had returned the previous evening, carrying boxes and bags filled with fresh, new, beautiful undergarments, stockings, petticoats, dresses, and hats, and the cobbler's son had presented them all with new shoes—when her sisters had squealed with joy and excitement over their new, luxurious wares—then Athena knew there was naught she could do but follow through with her agreement with Rafe.

Thus, there Athena sat with her sisters, riding toward the Dandridge home in the Dandridge carriage on Christmas Eve—riding toward her future and whatever it would bring.

As the coachman stopped the carriage and team in front of the Dandridges' home, Athena's heart began to beat with such anxiety that she was quite sure she would faint dead away for a moment. But she didn't, much to her surprise. And shortly the coachman was helping her sisters step down from the carriage one at a time.

Athena left the carriage lastly—perhaps because she knew a trepidation that soaked her to the soul, whereas her sisters knew only excitement.

Having obviously been watching through the windows for their arrival, it was Mrs. Dandridge who opened the front door and fairly glided down the steps toward them.

"Oh, my darlings, you've arrived at last!" Florence Dandridge exclaimed, fairly throwing her arms around Athena. "I told Rafe that you couldn't arrive fast enough for my liking. And it's Christmas Eve—what fun we shall have together!"

"Will we have Christmas biscuits, mum?" Bronwen asked.

"Hush, Bronwen," Annabel scolded.

But Mrs. Dandridge laughed, released her embrace of Athena, and leaned down to be face to face with Bronwen. "Of course, my angel! It wouldn't be Christmas Eve without Christmas biscuits, now would it?"

"No, mum, I think not," Bronwen giggled, smiling at her benefactress.

As Rafe appeared at the threshold of the house, Athena held her breath. He was so very tall, so very handsome, so very gallant looking in his finery for the holidays. As he descended the steps toward the place his mother stood greeting Athena and her sisters, Athena blushed when Mrs. Dandridge turned to him, calling, "Rafe! Your beautiful bride-to-be has arrived at last, and with her sweet, pretty sisters. Come help us please."

"Of course, Mother," Rafe said, striding toward them.

Athena blushed when a man and woman, out for a wintry morning stroll, stopped, the woman exclaiming, "Oh, my dear Mrs. Dandridge! Do my ears deceive me? Or did I hear you say only just now that your eldest son has at last found a bride?"

Terror washed over Athena as, once again, the remnants of her pride manifested themselves within her. Would Mrs. Dandridge reveal all to her acquaintance? Would she tell her friend that her son had chosen to wed a destitute pauper as penance for what he felt were his father's sins?

"Indeed, Mrs. Fernsworth," Mrs. Dandridge replied, however. "This is Miss Athena Monroe," she said, stepping aside and nodding toward Athena.

"Good morning, Mrs. Fernsworth," Athena greeted with a slight curtsy. "How pleased I am to meet you."

Mrs. Fernsworth studied Athena a moment, her smile broadening with approval. "And I you, Miss Monroe," the woman said. "It would seem our Rafe has found a lovely prize indeed in winning your hand."

"Thank you, mum," Athena managed, still blushing vermillion.

"And these darlings are Athena's sisters," Mrs. Dandridge explained, radiant with an obvious and sincere delight that quite puzzled Athena. "We're going in to eat Christmas biscuits, wassail, cheese, and anything else my darlings want. So we'll have to bid you good day, Mrs. Fernsworth…Mr. Fernsworth," Mrs. Dandridge said, nodding in turn to each of the Fernsworths.

"And good day to you, Mrs. Dandridge," Mrs. Fernsworth called as Mrs. Dandridge took Marta and Bronwen by the hands and led them toward the house.

"And congratulations are most certainly in order for you, Mr. Dandridge," Mr. Fernsworth said, tipping his hat to Athena.

"Yes, they are," Rafe said. He stepped aside and gestured that Annabel should precede him in following his mother into the house. Then with a good day to each of the Fernsworths in turn, Rafe took Athena's kid-gloved hand, placing it in the crook of his arm, and began escorting her toward the house.

"Good day," Athena said, nodding to the Fernsworths as they stood on the cobbles gawking in astonishment.

As they ascended the steps, Athena could not help but note how firm and solid Rafe's arm was where her hand rested on it. She could sense the slight scents of soap, leather, and fresh-ironed cotton about him, and an impish sensation of pride in the Fernsworths' seeing her in his company welled in her for a moment.

"We're so delighted that you're all finally here, Miss Monroe," Mrs. Dandridge exclaimed as Rafe escorted Athena into the parlor with the others. "I was simply beside myself with impatience this morning." Smiling at Athena and then to each of her sisters in return, Mrs. Dandridge continued, "Now do take off your wraps and settle in. Wentworth will bring in your bags once he's seen to the horses and carriage. Meanwhile, what's say we have a pastry or two, hmm?"

"Pastries? Truly?" Marta exclaimed with excitement.

Mrs. Dandridge laughed wholeheartedly. "Yes, darling! Yes! I'm quite a lover of pastries, you see."

"Me too," Bronwen chimed in.

"Miss Monroe?" Rafe said as he placed his hands on Athena's fur wrap at her shoulders. "May I?"

"Oh…oh, of course," Athena stammered. As Rafe removed her fur, she forced an awkward smile and said, "Thank you."

Rafe placed Athena's fur over the back of a chair in one corner of the parlor.

Then his mother said, "Girls, just hand your wraps to Rafe, and follow me to the kitchen… wherein pastries await for us to nibble on to our little hearts' content."

Giggling, Marta and Bronwen quickly unfastened their own wraps, placing them in Rafe's outstretched hand. Rafe added their small furs to Athena's and then caused Annabel's cheeks to pink with a delighted blush as he removed her fur in the same manner he had removed Athena's.

"Thank you, Mr. Dandridge," Annabel said to him, smiling and blushing with obvious pleasure.

"Rafe, if you don't mind, Miss Annabel," Rafe said, returning Annabel's smile.

Athena was surprised at the slight twinge of jealousy that suddenly invaded her thoughts. She did not like the fact that Rafe had smiled at Annabel in such a casual, friendly manner. After all, he had yet to smile at her that way, and she was meant to be his wife.

Placing one hand to her temple to ease a sudden ache there, Athena inwardly scolded herself. She was simply overly tired, and therefore her temperament was not as it should be.

"Are you feeling all right, Miss Monroe?" Rafe asked.

Shaking her head slightly to dispel the odd sense of slight dizziness in her, Athena smiled at him, answering, "Yes. Just a bit tired, I think. I did not sleep very well last night."

As Annabel followed Mrs. Dandridge, Marta, and Bronwen out of the parlor, Athena began to follow as well. Rafe, however, took hold of her arm, stalling her.

"May I beg a moment of your time, Miss Monroe?" he asked.

"Of course, Mr. Dandridge," Athena answered.

"Call me Rafe, if you would please," Rafe said as he motioned for her to take a seat on the sofa.

"Athena would please me as well," Athena told him.

"Very well, Athena," he said, taking a seat next to her. He grinned at her—a kind, understanding, yet slightly amused grin, as he said, "You're uncomfortable here." It was a statement, not a question.

"Yes," Athena admitted, feeling somehow bashful under his gaze.

"Don't be," Rafe said. "It's your home, and you do not have to make any pretenses. You don't have to pretend to be in love with me or that you're not disappointed in the lot life has thrust upon you. I would ask, however, that you try very hard to be as happy as you can be, given the circumstances. That's all I wish for you, Athena—comfort and happiness. Very well?"

"But it's such a strange situation," Athena confessed. "I...I didn't know it would be so awkward...though I suppose I should've known."

"Well, tomorrow we will wed, and then maybe you will begin to feel more at home," Rafe said. "After all, as my wife, you will have claim on this house and anything else that is mine. And if it helps at all for you to know that this house is indeed mine and not my mother's...then you have that as well."

Athena looked at him—studied the sincerity in his handsome countenance. "I am forever in your debt, Mr....Rafe," she said quietly. "And I will do all in my power to thank you at every turn for what you have done for my sisters and me."

"Then be comfortable in my home and happy in your new lot," he told her. "You sit where you want to sit, eat what you want to eat, read what books inspire you to read them, and dote on your sisters." He smiled. "And it might help you also to know that my mother is entirely out of her head with excitement over having four daughters all at once, as she put it to me."

Athena smiled, nodding as she said, "I can see that Marta and Bronwen have taken to her like hummingbirds to nectar already. They talked of nothing else but her beauty, kindness, wood fire, and Christmas biscuits after we left here the other night." Her smile broadened as she added, "They will steal your heart soon enough as well, no doubt."

Rafe grinned, and a quiet chuckle escaped his throat. "They are quite too adorable for their own good."

"Yes, they are," Athena agreed.

"And what of Annabel?" he asked. "Is she as irritable and hard to please as most girls of her tender age and heart?"

Athena giggled then, nodding and admitting, "At times. But she has been turned topsy-turvy once or twice in her young life."

"And so have you," Rafe suggested.

Athena again nodded. "Yes. But I am the eldest, and as you know, the eldest child in a family does not often know the luxury of thinking of his- or herself first above anything else. Isn't that right?"

Rafe's eyes narrowed as he studied her a moment. He understood her implication perfectly. She could read it in his countenance. He understood that she knew he was sacrificing as much as she was in marrying—perhaps more, for his choice could've been any woman, but hers was contingent on his mercy and charitable, self-sacrificing actions.

"Perhaps finishing school away for a time would help Annabel see the importance of a loving older sister and sweet younger ones, hmmm?" Rafe suggested. "You attended Prominence for Young Ladies, did you not? What was your experience?"

"I could not wait to return home," Athena admitted, again smiling up at him. "Like Annabel, I thought I would want to leave home, to attend Prominence and learn all the details of being a well-mannered, poised young woman. But the truth is, I only longed to return home to my family."

Rafe nodded. "Well then, you consider it for Annabel. Perhaps discuss the option with her and then let me know what you would like to do for her. I am more than happy to pay for her tuition and time there."

"You are very kind and overly benevolent, Rafe," Athena said as her heart swelled with gratitude.

"I am only trying to do right by you and yours that have been wronged by me and mine, Athena," Rafe said. "Now, what's say we join the others in the kitchen for some of those Christmas pastries before Mother nibbles them all gone herself, hmm?"

"Very well," Athena said as she stood. She paused in leaving the room, however—paused to gaze into the warm, crackling wood fire in the hearth. "I can promise that I will not miss the coal fires of Camden Town."

"Wood is a luxury that I admittedly spoil myself with," Rafe said. "I'm pleased to know you will enjoy it as well."

He took her hand then, placing it in the crook of his arm as they started toward the kitchen.

Smiling as they walked, Rafe said, "From the sounds of merriment wafting our way, you would think Mother had the girls into the rum."

Athena laughed, for the laughter emanating from the kitchen was a happy sound indeed.

Athena's eyes were heavy as she lay in the soft, warm, ever-so-snug bed. Wood embers still smoldered in the hearth of the bedchamber she was sharing with Annabel, and the melodic sound of the carols she and her sisters had sung while gathered around the pianoforte as Mrs. Dandridge played still echoed in her mind like a distant dream that lingers.

Marta and Bronwen were tucked in together in Mrs. Dandridge's room, and it soothed Athena beyond words to know that they were snug and warm, as she and Annabel were. She hoped Mrs. Dandridge was comfortable in Fenton's room upstairs—the one across from Rafe's—where she had decided to spend the night so that the Dandridge girls could have her rooms downstairs.

The wind howled past the bedchamber window, and though the sound of it caused a bit of anxiety to rise in Athena, the fact that warm quilts, fire embers, and strong walls of brick kept the cold bite of it at bay was consoling indeed. And she drifted off to slumber on Christmas Eve, warm, hopeful, and with quite unexpected, yet pleasant, visions of Rafe Dandridge dancing in her head.

# CHAPTER FIVE

"Wake up, Athena! Wake up! Mrs. Dandridge said Father Christmas has been here and that he brought something wonderful for Marta and me!"

It was Bronwen's sweet voice, filled with excitement, that drew Athena from the deepest sleep she'd known in months. Struggling to force her eyes open, she did smile, however, mumbling, "Father Christmas?"

"Yes! It's Christmas morning, silly!" Bronwen giggled. "Annabel and the others are all waiting in the kitchen for you and me to join them. Then Mrs. Dandridge says we can go into the parlor and see what Father Christmas has left. Hurry and get up, Athena!"

"All right, all right, darling," Athena giggled, amused by Bronwen's exhilaration. "Let me wash my face and get dressed, and then we'll—"

"No, no, no, Athena," Bronwen interrupted, however. "Mrs. Dandridge says we all must stay in our nightgowns and robes. That's how the Dandridges do their Christmas morning. So up, up, up, big sister! Wash your face, put on your lovely new robe over your lovely new nightgown, and come with me. Hurry! Quick as a rabbit!"

But Athena frowned as she sat up in bed. "Bronwen, we can't possibly go traipsing about in our nightdresses and robes, not with Mr. Dandridge present."

Bronwen shrugged. "Why not? Mr. Dandridge is already downstairs, and he's only wearing long underwear, his robe, and slippers."

"What?" Athena exclaimed.

"Oh, that reminds me," Bronwen said as she bent down beside Athena's bed for a moment. "Mrs. Dandridge had me bring these for you!" Standing erect once more, Bronwen stood, holding a lovely pair of fleece-lined slippers in her hands in offering.

"Mrs. Dandridge says we all must have slippers so our feet are not cold on winter mornings," Bronwen explained. "See?" she said, lifting her own slippered foot to show Athena. "They're so very soft, Athena! And I swear my feet have never been so cozy and warm." Taking hold of Athena's hand then, Bronwen urged, "Now hurry, Athena! Everyone is waiting for us, and I can hardly endure another moment of waiting!"

Though it all seemed highly improper, Athena did as her little sister instructed. Quickly washing her face and smoothing her hair she'd braided the night before (for Bronwen would not allow her the time to rebraid it), Athena put on the beautiful robe Mrs. Dandridge had given her the night before, slipped on the warm, fleece-lined slippers, and followed her little sister to the kitchen.

Athena's eyes widened as she and Bronwen joined the others, for indeed everyone—including Mrs. Dandridge and Rafe—wore their bed-wear and robes.

"Oh, at last, darling!" Mrs. Dandridge exclaimed as they entered. "We've been quite beside ourselves with anticipation, Athena." Mrs. Dandridge smiled at Marta. "We tried to be patient—to let you rest—but our selfishness got the better of us. Isn't that right, Rafe?"

Athena could not help but smile as Rafe—who had been sitting in a chair at the table, resting his head on his folded arms—raised his head, sat up straight in his chair, and, with his tousled hair giving him the look of a schoolboy, said, "Yes, that's right." He grinned at Athena with understanding, adding, "None of us could sleep another wink."

Athena giggled, delighted by his boyish appearance and his sleepy sarcasm.

"You should have woken me sooner," she said as she looked to each face in the room—each face that was bright with anticipation. Even Rafe appeared less severe—more relaxed and cheerful.

"That's what I kept saying," Marta said, exhaling with impatience.

"Well, you're here now, Athena," Mrs. Dandridge said. "So who wants to race to the parlor with me to see what Father Christmas has left for us, hmmm?"

"Me!" Bronwen and Marta chimed in unison.

Annabel smiled at Athena as Mrs. Dandridge and the girls scampered ahead of them. "Come along, Athena," Annabel said. "Perhaps Father Christmas left something for you and me as well."

"Oh, I can promise you that he did," Rafe said, rising from his chair and raking a hand back though his hair. "And I'm quite certain he was awake most of the night preparing it."

As squeals of pure joy erupted from the parlor, Annabel giggled, "I'm not waiting another moment for you, Athena," as she hurried off toward the sounds of exuberance.

Athena paused, however, touching Rafe's arm as he strode near to her. "Thank you, Mr. Dandridge."

"Rafe," he corrected her with a kind grin. "And for what?"

Athena smiled. "For slathering me and my sisters in kindness and gifts."

But Rafe shrugged, saying, "It was Father Christmas's doing, not mine."

"Was it?" Athena giggled.

"Of course," Rafe assured her. Taking her hand then, he placed it in the crook of his arm. "Come now. Let's see if Father Christmas has left anything for you and me, hmm?"

"But we're grown-ups," Athena reminded him as they started toward the parlor. "Father Christmas only visits for the sake of children."

Rafe frowned, feigning astonishment. "Father Christmas has visited me every year for as far back as my memory allows…and still does. I hope your lack of faith in him doesn't find you with a lump of coal in your stocking, Athena Monroe."

Athena's heart swelled—swelled with happiness in finding that Rafe Dandridge did indeed have a playful side to his otherwise brooding and intimidating character. She was secretly very relieved to discern it, for as she was going to spend her entire life with him, she knew it would be far more pleasant a thing to do knowing he had a wit and sense of humor.

As Athena stepped into the parlor, the sight that met her caused her to gasp in awe—brought tears to her eyes for the splendor of it all!

As Mrs. Dandridge and Annabel sat on the parlor sofa, Marta and Bronwen were jubilant in their detailed investigation of the most perfectly detailed, beautiful dollhouse Athena had ever imagined! And even more breathtaking than the lavish dollhouse Father Christmas had left for the girls was the resplendent Christmas tree he had placed in one corner of the parlor. The large evergreen boasted lit candles on its branches and was laden with small gifts wrapped in brown paper and tied with crimson velvet ribbons. Beneath its lowest boughs sat an intricately carved Noah's ark, surrounded by like artistically crafted and painted wooden animals and a literal multitude of larger gifts, wrapped like those small ones that adorned the tree's boughs.

Athena found that her breath was quite taken away by the dazzling beauty and welcoming sight of the Dandridges' parlor so bedecked with Christmas cheer. Plates piled with pastries, biscuits, canapés, mincemeat, and Christmas pudding looked near to spilling over as they crowded Mrs. Dandridge's parlor table. A warm, crackling wood fire burned in the hearth, and its soothing fragrance, blended with that of the evergreen in the room, was akin to intoxicating, and Athena was overwhelmed by the sensation of being carried into a dream.

"It's…it's far too much," Athena whispered. She felt dizzy—found herself using Rafe's arm to keep from faltering to her knees. Looking up at Rafe, she repeated, "It's far too much. You didn't need to do all this for us."

But Rafe frowned, again feigning ignorance. "Don't scold me about it. It's Father Christmas's doing."

"Oh, come see, come see, Athena!" Marta exclaimed. "There are little framed paintings on the walls of this dollhouse, velvet chairs to sit the dolls in, beds with tiny quilts! Do come see this!"

"You too, Annabel," Bronwen coaxed. "Come play with us!" Bronwen quickly scurried over to Mrs. Dandridge, taking hold of both of her hands. "Won't you play with us too, mum? There is a whole family of dolls within the house...even a dainty little Christmas tree in its parlor. Come and see!"

Mrs. Dandridge laughed, delighted by the invitation to join the fun. "Of course, I'll play!" the woman giggled as she followed Bronwen to the dollhouse. "What fun we shall have, hmmm?"

"You better join them for a while," Rafe said to Athena. He removed her hand from his arm, nodding toward the dollhouse. "The day is young...very young," he added, stifling a yawn. "I'll simply deposit myself on the sofa for a time, rest a bit while you ladies squeal over the delights Father Christmas has left for you."

"Very well," Athena said—though she felt as tired yet as Rafe looked to be. "We wouldn't want Father Christmas to think us ungrateful for his efforts, after all, would we?"

Rafe grinned. "Indeed not."

"Come along, Athena!" Marta called. "We've got just the doll for you!"

As the joy of the morning began to truly sink into Athena's consciousness then, she smiled at Rafe once more and then joined her sisters and Mrs. Dandridge at the dollhouse.

As she knelt down at the back of the dollhouse with the others and began peeking into each room—awed by the intricately crafted miniature furniture, linens, and all inside—Bronwen said, "Here, Athena. This can be your doll."

Athena gasped, surprised when her little sister handed her a small doll dressed in a bridal gown and veil.

"We thought it quite appropriate that you should play with the bride doll," Mrs. Dandridge explained, smiling, "being that this is your wedding day, as well as Christmas."

"Yes," Athena whispered. "Yes…I suppose it is."

"Come now," Mrs. Dandridge said, placing a comforting arm across Athena's shoulders. "No worries or cares just now. Let's enjoy our morning and all the bounty Father Christmas has bestowed on us in remembrance of the birth of our Lord, all right?"

Determining to enjoy the bounty, the blessing of rescue heaped upon her family, Athena nodded and said, "Yes, mum."

"Is every Christmas like this one at your house, mum?" Marta asked as she sat beside Mrs. Dandridge on the sofa later in the day.

Mrs. Dandridge laughed. "Oh my goodness, no! I think Father Christmas simply recognized that this was our first Christmas all together as a new family, and he wanted it to be memorable…and very special."

"Well, I for one will never forget it," Marta sighed. She looked to Athena then, adding, "More gifts and food than I ever could have imagined in all my life. And now Athena looks so beautiful in that gown, and we are to have a wedding—right here, in this house, on Christmas Day. I shall never forget a moment of this!"

"Nor shall I, darling," Mrs. Dandridge said, placing an affectionate kiss to Marta's temple.

"Are you all right, Athena?" Annabel asked in a whisper as she fussed over Athena's gown. "You look a little pale."

"Do I?" Athena almost snapped. "Well, could it be for the sake that I'm about to bind myself—my life…and for the whole of my life—to a man I barely know?"

Annabel frowned. "But Mrs. Dandridge said you have known Rafe almost all your life…and he you."

Athena nodded—tried to breathe evenly. "We grew up near one another, the families living very close to one another. But Rafe always frightened me a bit…especially when I was just a girl. It was Fenton, his younger brother, that I knew best."

Annabel stared at her older sister a moment and then, placing her hands on Athena's shoulders, said, "You don't have to marry him, Athena. We will survive without them…or their money."

"I know," Athena said. "But surviving would be all that we would do. We would not thrive… especially Marta and Bronwen." She swallowed the lump of trepidation that had gathered in her throat. "And Rafe…he was always the steadfast one. He will take care of all of us. His word is proof of that. He is an honorable man."

Annabel smiled. "And the most handsome man I have ever seen."

Athena smiled as well, amused by her sister's obvious admiration of Rafe's charming good looks. "Yes. He is that."

Annabel reached down, fluffing out the skirt of Athena's wedding dress. "And he got this right, didn't he? The perfect gown for you...even though you're being married here and not in some grand cathedral. He chose the most elegant wedding gown I have ever seen in all my life!"

Athena blushed. "Yes. It seems rather foolhardy, doesn't it? Such a gown for such a small, short ceremony." Athena giggled nervously. "It hardly fits in the parlor!"

Athena gasped a little as she heard the front door open. A moment later, a curate entered, followed by Rafe.

"Oh my!" the curate—a short, friendly looking man with a pair of spectacles balanced on the end of his nose—said upon seeing Athena. "You did not tell me your bride was so beautiful, Mr. Dandridge."

"Welcome, Vicar Bowers," Mrs. Dandridge greeted, fairly hopping up from the sofa. "We are so very glad you could perform the ceremony today!"

"May I speak with you privately a moment, Athena?" Rafe said as he approached Athena.

"Of course," Athena said—though every anxiety and fear she had ever known began to course through her veins. Had Rafe changed his mind, decided not to take pity on Athena and her sisters? Would they find themselves stripped of all the beautiful comforts, warmth, clothing, food, and gifts that Father Christmas had left them—returned to ruin and misery and cold?

"I have something for you," Rafe said, however. Reaching into his coat pocket, he retrieved a small, varnished, wooden box. Offering it to her, he explained, "This is for you…a gift from your groom."

Athena smiled and laughed a little, saying, "Whatever for? Did not Father Christmas leave everything any of us could ever have dreamed of in your parlor to be found this morning?"

Rafe smiled and nodded. "Perhaps he did. But those gifts were from Father Christmas. This one is from me."

Athena looked at the box a moment—at the manner in which Rafe held it out in offering it to her. Then, with a trembling hand, she reached out and accepted it.

"Open it please," Rafe instructed.

Athena did open it, and as she did, she gasped—delighted by both the music that began by way of the music box inlaid in it and the gold and diamond wedding ring that lay inside.

"It-it's beautiful!" Athena breathed. "All of it! The box, the music…and…and…"

"It is your wedding ring," Rafe needlessly explained. "I hope it is to your liking."

"Oh, it is!" Athena exclaimed. She was thoroughly overwhelmed—dizzyingly so—and she teetered a bit from side to side.

Reaching to steady her by taking hold of her arms, Rafe frowned, asking, "Are you indeed well, Athena?"

"Yes…yes, of course," she assured him. "It's simply…all of it, the past two days…it's simply so much to take in is all. And now this?" She smiled, tears brimming in her eyes. "You go too far with your charitable contributions, Rafe."

But Rafe's frown deepened. "These are not charitable contributions, Athena," he almost growled. "You are to be my wife…and I will treat you as a wife should be treated. Do you understand?"

"I understand you are quite different than I judged you to be when I was a child," she humbly and guiltily admitted.

Though Rafe's frown softened, he did not seem at ease. Turning to the curate, he said, "Vicar Bowers, if you are ready…Miss Monroe and I are."

As was becoming his habit—and Athena recognized that it was a gesture of reassurance and support—Rafe took her hand, placing it in the crook of his arm.

"Very well," Vicar Bowers said, smiling. "If the witnesses are present, we will begin."

Athena was astonished at the manner in which Charles—the serving man she had seen the night she and her sisters had come caroling—seemed to appear out of nowhere. He was wearing his everyday clothes, not his serving uniform, and he nodded to Rafe and Rafe to him.

Mrs. Dandridge stood and strode to where they all stood in the parlor as well. She too nodded to Rafe and he to her.

"Everything is at the ready," Rafe said to the vicar.

"Wonderful!' Vicar Bowers exclaimed. "Then, if you will please take Miss Monroe's hands in yours, Rafe…I will marry you to her."

Dizziness such as Athena had never before experienced took hold in her head then. In truth, she but barely managed to repeat her own wedding vows—to keep her attention steady on Rafe as she did so. So quick was the ceremony, in fact, that Athena's head still felt as if it were spinning as she heard the vicar say, "You may kiss your bride, Mr. Dandridge." She barely felt Rafe's lips press the back of her hand—barely managed to sign her name to her own wedding papers and watch Charles and Mrs. Dandridge sign theirs as witnesses.

Somehow she managed to return the loving embraces of each of her sisters' congratulatory hugs, and that of Mrs. Dandridge.

But it was the opening of the front door—the appearance of the unexpected guest—that sent Athena's mind to being far too overwhelmed with change and relief in her sisters' security—and sent Athena swooning into a faint.

The front door opened, and Fenton Dandridge entered—tall and handsome like his elder brother, but with a countenance as nearly completely opposite as two brothers' countenances could be—Fenton Dandridge, a far more familiar Dandridge to Athena than any other. As Fenton entered the parlor, throwing his arms wide and proclaiming, "Happy Christmas to all!" Athena felt the room begin to spin.

Fenton, still smiling, arched his brows, however, and looking directly at Athena asked, "And what's all this, might I ask?"

It was the last thing Athena would remember about her wedding day—her last vision being that of Rafe gazing with concern into her face and scooping her up into the cradle of his powerful arms an instant before the darkness of unconsciousness claimed her.

# CHAPTER SIX

Athena tried to open her eyes—tried very hard. But no matter how many times she told herself to wake up, to open her eyes and respond to the conversation seeping into her mind, she just could not quite achieve full consciousness. She felt as if full wakefulness were only an arm's length away but that her arms weren't long enough to grasp hold of it.

"Well," a man's voice that was unfamiliar to her was saying, "at first, I thought perhaps it was a case of 'bashful bride.' But it seems to me to be more an issue of extreme exhaustion."

"What's bashful bride, Mrs. Dandridge?" Athena heard Marta inquire.

Athena heard Fenton's all-too-recognizable chuckle as Mrs. Dandridge said, "Annabel, why don't you and the littler girls see to that lovely Noah's ark Father Christmas left for you, hmm?"

"Yes, mum," Annabel said. "Come along, girls. The doctor will tend to Athena, and she'll be right as rain in no time at all."

"Perhaps she took one look at me when I appeared and realized she'd married the wrong Dandridge brother," Fenton said.

"And you may take yourself into the kitchen, Fenton Dandridge," Mrs. Dandridge ordered. "I swear in all my life I've never seen anyone with a worse sense of when to arrive than you."

"Oh, don't be cross with me, Mother," Fenton said coolly. "Athena will rally. She always does."

"To the kitchen, Fenton…now," Mrs. Dandridge repeated.

"Your bride is very thin, Mr. Dandridge," noted the voice of the unfamiliar man, who Athena surmised was a doctor. "Perhaps she has let herself starve in being worried to fit into her wedding gown."

"Perhaps," Athena heard Rafe mumble.

"Still, exhaustion is my diagnosis," the doctor pronounced. "She'll be fine in a few days. But she needs rest, complete rest, and plenty of warm broth and water."

"Yes, Doctor," Mrs. Dandridge said.

"I'd suggest you take her to her room—upstairs would be best. Undress her and put her to bed," the doctor said further. "Wake her morning, midday, and evenings to make sure she eats something and drinks enough. But I think that is all that is needed." There was a pause where no one spoke. Then the doctor, in a very lowered voice, said, "I'm afraid consummation of the marriage will have to be put off for a few nights."

"Of course, of course," Rafe said quietly.

"She's a beautiful young woman, Mr. Dandridge," the doctor said. "Congratulations on your nuptials."

"Thank you, Doctor," Rafe rather grumbled.

"Well, I'll be on my way then," the doctor said. "Send for me if anything changes or if you have any concerns."

"Thank you, Doctor," Mrs. Dandridge said, as well. "I hope you won't mind if Charles sees you out."

"Not at all. Not at all," the doctor said.

"I'm sorry to have kept you from your family this long, Charles," Rafe's voice boomed. "Please hurry home as soon as you've seen the doctor out. And here's something for your trouble today. Happy Christmas, Charles."

"Happy Christmas to you, Mr. Dandridge!" Charles exclaimed.

Athena discerned the clinking of coins changing hands and knew that Rafe had paid Charles handsomely for his sacrifice on Christmas Day.

"Let's get her upstairs to your room at once, Rafe," Mrs. Dandridge said. "We must undress her and put her to bed."

As Athena felt Rafe's strong arms move beneath her—felt herself being lifted into them, cradled against his chest—she again tried to push herself to full wakefulness. But the only result was a long, quiet moan escaping her throat.

"It's no wonder," Mrs. Dandridge said as Athena felt Rafe climbing the stairs. "The girl has been working her fingers to the bone for some taskmaster in a kitchen somewhere...so Annabel tells me. Annabel says Athena doesn't eat well either, giving everything to her sisters and saving only the thinnest broth for herself. It's truly a miracle the girl was able to stand long enough to exchange vows with you, Rafe."

"Yes…so it would seem," Rafe said.

Athena experienced a sudden sense of blissfulness as the warmth of Rafe's breath caressed her face as he carried her. All at once, though she still could not wake herself, she felt rather euphoric.

"And then Fenton! Of all people to arrive at that moment," Mrs. Dandridge grumbled. "I think the shock of seeing Fenton again, after all this time, was the end of her endurance."

"It's a feeling with which I can commiserate, Mother," Rafe said.

"Here, lay her on the bed, darling, and help me get her gown and things off, please," Mrs. Dandridge said.

At the idea that Rafe would be present while her clothes were being removed, Athena silently screamed to her body to wake up! Yet again, all that occurred was another moan.

"Hold her up, darling," Mrs. Dandridge suggested. "Sit her up on the bed, and I'll unbutton the dress bodice."

It was the sense of her head on his shoulder, the masculine aroma of leather and soap, that worked to wake her then.

"I-I can do it myself," Athena managed to speak—though her eyes remained closed.

"Can you stand?" Rafe asked.

"I-I think so," Athena answered. Yet as she attempted to stand, she found her strength was entirely drained from her.

"Hold here a moment," Rafe said, pulling her body against his.

Athena could feel Mrs. Dandridge working the buttons at the back of her gown, and when her bodice opened at the back, she felt the laces of her corset go slack—her petticoat loosen at her waist.

"Now then, darling," Mrs. Dandridge began, "pull her out of it all as I tug it all down, yes?"

Athena felt her gown slip down over her arms and then from her body completely. She felt Rafe's powerful arms at the back of her knees and around her back once more as he lifted her out of her clothing. She was entirely embarrassed! She could feel Rafe's bare hands on her back and at the bend of her knees with only her camisole and bloomers between his skin and hers. And yet there was a bigger part of her that felt comforted by his touch—safe and secure in his arms and against his protective body.

"Put her to bed now, Rafe dear," Mrs. Dandridge instructed softly.

As Athena felt her body being laid gently on soft sheet, she whispered, "I'm so sorry, Rafe."

"Rest well, my darling," Mrs. Dandridge said. Athena felt a soft, moist kiss to her forehead—a mother's kiss, something she hadn't known in a very long time—and it caused tears to escape her weary, still-closed eyes.

"You will be watched over, Athena." It was Rafe—and the strength and promise in his voice soothed her further. "Your sisters will be well cared for. So rest now."

Athena sensed the sheet, followed by the quilt, as someone covered her. The soft pillow under her head was the last thing she remembered thinking of before deep sleep consumed her.

Though Athena slept deeply that Christmas, she did not sleep peacefully. Rather she slept fitfully, for her dreams were laced with fear, worry, and memories of her parents' death and their coming to Camden Town to live. In her dreams, Mr. Eads yelled harsh words at her and criticized her work, and Annabel, Marta, and

Bronwen were naught but skin and bones for lack of nourishment.

One nightmare was so powerful that Athena burst to consciousness, crying out with the revisited grief of her mother's death. But as she brushed tears from her cheeks with weak hands, she saw that Mrs. Dandridge was sitting at the foot of her bed.

The maternal-looking woman smiled and whispered, "Shhh. All is well, Athena. All is well," and held her hand until sleep claimed Athena once again.

Although the next morning found Athena wakeful, she was weak—profoundly weak. Hardly able to do any more than attend to her necessaries and sip a little broth and milk, she did at least sleep more easily when Bronwen joined her in her bed for a midday nap.

The night, however, brought the return of her nightmares, and she woke once or twice sobbing and feeling ill. This time, however, it was not Mrs. Dandridge sitting at the foot of her bed—but rather Rafe in a chair next to it. And although his voice did not have the same effect of soothing that Mrs. Dandridge's had, it comforted her in quite a different manner.

"Your sisters are well and warm, Athena," Rafe said each time. "You are safe. I will watch over you, so sleep in knowing all is well tonight."

Rafe's voice stayed with her—visited her dreams—and Athena began to rest, truly rest, to recover.

On the third day following her wedding to Rafe, she bathed in the large copper tub in Rafe's room that Mrs. Dandridge had prepared for her. And after Annabel had brushed her hair dry before the fire, Marta and Bronwen chose a day dress, from the large collection of dresses and gowns that Mrs. Dandridge had given her for Christmas, and helped her dress.

By the time supper was to be served, Athena felt more alive and like herself once more, and she joined the others in the dining room.

Athena was surprised when she entered the dining room, however, to see Mrs. Dandridge sitting at one side of the table with Annabel, Marta, and Bronwen across from them, instead of at the foot of the table opposite Rafe.

Standing when she entered the room, Rafe strode to the foot of the table and assisted Athena in sitting.

"But...but isn't this your place, Mrs. Dandridge?" Athena asked—for she was quite unsettled at being seated where she was.

Mrs. Dandridge laughed, tossing a wave to the air. "Oh, goodness no, darling! You're mistress of this house. It is your seat."

"Are you feeling quite well?" Rafe asked unexpectedly.

Athena looked to the head of the table where he sat, frowning with concern.

"I am," Athena answered. Then bowing her head with the bearing of humiliation, she added, "And I do so want to apologize for all the trouble and worry I've caused you." She glanced up, looking from Rafe to his mother. "All of you. I-I don't know what overcame me. I...I..."

"The doctor Rafe brought said he thought, at first, you had a case of bashful bride," Marta said. "But you didn't...or so the doctor determined. Yet no one will tell me what a case of bashful bride is, Athena! And I've been so frustrated with curiosity in waiting to ask you. What is a case of bashful bride, Athena?"

As Athena's cheeks burned crimson, everyone else at the table, including Rafe, stared at her with expectation.

"You see, Athena," Rafe began, "Marta has explained to us all, several times, that you never skirt a question she asks you. Marta and Bronwen, and Annabel also, have assured Mother and me that once you were rested and well, you would not pause in putting sweet Marta's curiosity to respite."

"Isn't it true, Athena?" Bronwen said. "You always answer our questions."

"Yes, I do," Athena rather gulped. "However, this is an inquiry that may be better discussed in private."

"Why?" Marta asked then. "Mrs. Dandridge says we are all family now. And it is you, Athena, who has always said keeping secrets is a trick indeed."

Rafe grinned at Athena with understanding—and amusement. "I agree. We are a family now. So why should you pause in answering Marta's question? Do tell us, Athena…what is a case of bashful bride?"

Mrs. Dandridge giggled a little into the handkerchief she'd been holding.

"Very well," Athena began, inhaling a breath of courage.

"A bashful bride is a woman who has just been married," she began, "and is quite uncomfortable or shy about...about...about marital sleeping arrangements that are...that are..."

"That are new and different to her, as it were," Rafe kindly interjected.

Marta frowned and exchanged glances of confusion with Bronwen. "I still don't understand," she said.

"Oh, for pity's sake, Marta!" Annabel exclaimed with exasperation. "A bashful bride is one who is nervous because, instead of sleeping in her own bed, she now must share her husband's bed! The doctor thought that Athena was bashful about sharing a bed with Rafe now that they are married!"

Marta shrugged. "But we girls all slept in one bed in Camden Town. So why would the doctor think you were nervous about sharing a bed with Rafe, Athena?"

"Enough, Marta," Annabel sighed with exasperation. "You have your answer about what a case of bashful bride is—thank heaven, for you've been at us for days over it. And now it's someone else's turn to add to our dinner conversation." Smiling, Annabel added, "What's say I go first?"

"Oh, so you have a question for me as well?" Athena asked. Though she was quite glad to be done with the discomfort Marta's curiosity was causing her, Athena was a bit afraid Annabel might cause her humiliation from another venue.

"No," Annabel assured her. "I just think it's so sad that you've missed so much, Athena," she explained. "I mean, you missed dinner Christmas night and all the visiting. Fenton stayed on for supper after you fainted, and we all found him quite delightful, didn't we?"

When no one agreed with her, including Bronwen and Marta, Annabel continued, "Oh, that's right. He spent most of his time talking with me."

Athena was very disquieted at Annabel's obvious admiration of Fenton. She knew Fenton Dandridge all too well—knew his charming, wily ways. And when she glanced up to Rafe to find him looking at her, wearing an expression of disquiet of his own, Athena was relieved that she was not alone in her worry.

"Oh, how we talked, Athena!" Annabel giggled.

Mrs. Dandridge stared down at her plate, her shoulders quite uncharacteristically slumped forward.

"Fenton is at university, you know, Athena," Annabel babbled, "and has so many friends and adventures to speak of."

"Which reminds me, Annabel," Athena interjected, "in my absence, did Rafe mention to you the possibility of your attending Prominence?"

It was out of her mouth before she'd quite realized she'd said it, and Athena looked to Rafe to watch his reaction to what she'd blurted.

"Prominence?" Annabel asked, her excitement over Fenton Dandridge's charms forgotten in favor of thinking of Prominence. "No. No, he didn't," Annabel said. "Were you…were you really considering Prominence for me, Athena? Rafe?" she asked, looking from Athena to Rafe.

"Absolutely," Rafe confirmed.

Athena exhaled a sigh of relief in Rafe's support of her desperate babble. Athena knew what it was to be Fenton Dandridge's prey—knew what a cat he was to a girl mouse—and she had begun to worry the instant she saw the gleefulness in Annabel's expression when she spoke of him.

"Oh, Prominence Finishing for Young Ladies is an excellent school, Annabel!" Mrs. Dandridge chimed. Athena did not miss the way Mrs.

Dandridge's posture straightened when the subject turned from Fenton to Prominence. "I attended Prominence myself when I was your age. And what friends and fun I had there!"

"Oh, am I really going to attend Prominence, Athena? Truly?" Annabel asked with wild exuberance.

"Well, Rafe would have to be willing to—" Athena stammered.

"Of course you may attend, Annabel," Rafe finished for her. He smiled at Athena, and she knew he was thinking that it would be best to send Annabel away to Prominence—especially with her newfound infatuation with Fenton to consider. "I'll contact the headmistress at once. Perhaps you may begin as soon as the new year."

"Oh, Rafe!" Annabel squealed as she fairly leapt from her chair to throw her arms around Rafe's neck in appreciation. "Thank you! Thank you so much!"

Rafe smiled, chuckled, and nodding toward Athena said, "Thank your sister. It's her love and caring for you that finds you able to attend Prominence."

"Thank you, Athena!" Annabel chirped as she hurried to hug Athena. "And I'm so glad you're feeling better. You've missed so much, and I don't want you to miss any more."

"Yes...yes, I can see that," Athena said as she returned her sister's happy embrace.

And it was true. Athena sat feeling a bit resentful about the fact that her younger sister had had the opportunity to spend more time with Athena's new husband than Athena herself had.

"One doesn't realize how life goes on without them, when one is unable to be involved, I suppose," Athena said.

Mrs. Dandridge smiled with understanding at Athena, reached out, and covered her hand with her own. "Oh, you didn't miss so much, darling. Most of the time Rafe was sleeping in a chair right next to you." She winked, and Athena blushed.

Looking up to Rafe, she said, "I hope you know that it was an isolated moment of invalidism for me, Rafe. I...I'm not weak. I-I don't know why I—"

"I know why," Rafe interrupted, however. His eyes narrowed as he stared at her, and for some strange reason, his gaze caused goose pimples to prickle the back of Athena's neck and shoulders. "And so does Mother," he added. "So that is the last I will hear of apologies from you."

"But I feel so——" Athena began.

"Exhaustion, Athena," Rafe interrupted. "You succumbed to extreme exhaustion. And believe you me, it was no fault of yours."

"You're all better now, Athena," Bronwen offered. "So don't worry. From here on, you can sleep with Rafe every night."

Mrs. Dandridge laughed quietly, and Athena blushed when she looked up to Rafe, and he said, "That's right, little Bronwen. No case of bashful bride here."

"I wonder how Fenton will feel when he is told I will be leaving to attend Prominence," Annabel thought aloud.

Rafe exhaled a sigh of disgust and mumbled, "Yes. I will most certainly contact the headmistress as soon as possible."

Athena nodded her thanks to him—for it seemed he was to be the deliverer of not only their welfare but also Annabel's naïveté.

After dinner, as everyone sat in the parlor together attending to various interests and activities, Rafe looked to Athena from his seat in a large chair to where she sat next to Bronwen on the sofa.

"I must tell you, Athena," he began, "that I was quite certain that I might be a widower before I'd had the chance to be a husband when you fainted as you did."

"I'm so very sorry, Rafe," Athena began to apologize. "I think everything—the past year, Camden Town, Mr. Eads—I think I was just very, very tired."

"Come along, girls," Mrs. Dandridge said, rising from her own chair. "Come with me. I've so wanted to reread the books Father Christmas left for you. Come to my bedchamber, and we'll enjoy a nice mug of warm milk and some stories."

"May I come too, mum?" Annabel asked.

"Of course, darling. I meant for you to," Mrs. Dandridge said.

Athena blushed, knowing full well her mother-in-law was conspiring to offer her son and Athena some privacy.

After her sisters and Mrs. Dandridge had gone, Athena repeated, "I really am so very sorry, Rafe...and terribly humiliated. To drop dead in a faint the moment after one is married—what Vicar Bowers must have thought!"

Rafe smiled. "Well, I do admit to thinking that perhaps Fenton was right in his supposition."

"What supposition?" Athena asked—though in truth Fenton's remarks, while the doctor had been caring for Athena before she'd been moved to Rafe's bedchamber, had been a great part of the haunting, miserable nightmares she'd endured during her convalescing. Still, she did not want Rafe to know she knew of them. And so she feigned ignorance.

"Fenton suggested that it was he that caused your faint," Rafe explained, "that when he appeared, you instantly realized you'd wed the wrong brother, and your intense regret was what found you unconscious."

"Oh, poppycock," Athena grumbled, trying not to blush. "I hardly remember him arriving. In truth, if it must be known, my head was swirling before the curate had even arrived. I'd begun to think I was taking ill or that perhaps the mincemeat had not agreed with my digestion."

Rafe's gaze never left her, even as he said, "Well, it would be understandable. After all, I'm not ignorant to the fact that you were once very infatuated with my brother."

Athena thought of the incident of her adolescence—the day Rafe had come upon her and

Fenton as Fenton was about to steal a kiss from her. What Rafe didn't know was that the next day, Fenton did kiss her—and she had kissed him in return. Oh, nothing came of it, of course. In truth, she was rather disgusted by Fenton's slobbery kiss. But her deepest desire in that moment was that Rafe—the man who had rescued her from misery and certain ruination of one sort or another—never know what had transpired between her and Fenton years ago. Furthermore, she wanted him to know how grateful she was to him, how indebted she felt, and that she would strive to be a good, kind, caring, nurturing, and hopefully one day loving wife to him, in every regard.

"I was just a girl then...younger than Annabel is now," Athena began. "And we all of us know how charming your brother can be...beguiling just like the devil himself."

"It's no matter to me, Athena," Rafe chuckled, smiling. "We all of us had our infatuations to endure as youths."

"But it's important to me that you know where my loyalty lies, Rafe," she told him, "that I will never forget all you have done and are doing...and will do." Athena sighed, "Annabel's tuition to Prominence alone—it makes my stomach churn to think of it. I owe you so much, Rafe. So much more than I can ever give." She paused then, laughing. "And how pathetic am I? In owing you so much…and I couldn't even make it to our marriage bed the night of our wedding."

Rafe laughed as well. "Well, in truth, you did make it to our marriage bed. You were simply unconscious when you arrived."

Florence paused in her reading aloud to the girls when she heard Rafe's and Athena's laughter wafting into her bedchamber from the parlor. She smiled. Rafe would know happiness the like he'd never imagined with Athena at his side. Perhaps he did not love her yet, but he would. And Florence knew that Athena would love Rafe to a far greater depth than he could imagine.

"I wonder what they're laughing about," Marta said.

"Oh, it doesn't matter, does it? Their laughter means they are enjoying each other's company, and that is what is important," Florence answered. "Now let's continue, shall we?"

As Florence continued to read, she smiled, for her heart was warm in knowing there was healing in the house—healing, children, four new daughters for her to cherish, and great love on the horizon for her kind, honorable, and very deserving Rafe.

# CHAPTER SEVEN

The later the hour grew, the more anxious Athena became. As great as her desire was to please her Rafe—to prove to him her loyalty and intent to be a good, faithful, and capable wife—she did, in fact, have a severe case of bashful bride.

In truth, Athena knew only a bit of what transpired between a man and woman in their marriage bed—and only a very little bit. Athena knew nothing in detail of what Rafe would expect from her. It was one of the many, many, innumerable moments that she wished her mother were near, for as Athena had always tried to answer her sisters' questions without pause, so her mother had been the same. Her mother would have told Athena what to expect, how to behave, what would happen between Athena and Rafe.

She thought then of the doctor's words—of what he'd told Rafe when she had been fainted on the sofa. *I'm afraid consummation of the marriage will have to be put off for a few nights.* Athena's mother would have been able to explain to her all that was expected of "consummation." But her mother had not lived long enough to tell Athena all that was expected—all that marital intimacy required.

Therefore, as the clock struck ten—as Athena realized her sisters and Mrs. Dandridge had retired near two hours earlier—as Rafe yawned, stretched, and said, "Well, shall we retire, then?"—Athena's stomach wound itself into a knot of anxiety.

"Y-yes," she managed to stammer. "It is very late after all, isn't it?"

"Very," Rafe said. Standing, he grinned at her, and it was a grin of mischief—as if he knew her discomfort and was mildly amused by it. Holding one large, strong hand out to her, he said, "Are you coming with me?"

Placing her small hand in his large one, Athena began to tremble—for the warm power of his grasp was quite overwhelming in its pleasing quality.

"O-of course," Athena said, rising from her own seat.

Rafe held Athena's hand as he led her up the stairs. And the closer they drew to his bedchamber—to their bedchamber—the more Athena began to tremble.

Leading her into the bedchamber, Rafe closed the door behind them. Someone, most likely Charles, had already built a fire in the hearth, and the wood burned so hot that the room was almost uncomfortably warm.

Taking both her hands in his, Rafe's eyes narrowed, smoldering as he studied her. "Are you nervous, Athena?" he asked.

She considered fibbing to him—feigning courage. But instead she said, "Terrified, in truth."

Rafe laughed—wholeheartedly laughed. And when his laughter at last subsided, Athena's eyes widened as he began to unbutton his shirt.

"What do you know about the goings-on between man and wife, Athena?" he asked bluntly.

"I-I don't know what I know," Athena admitted.

Rafe grinned, his bronze eyes seeming to glow in the firelight. "You don't know what you know?" he inquired.

Athena bit her lower lip, glancing away shyly as Rafe stripped off his shirt to reveal his bare torso beneath. Although Athena had not seen many men in such a state of undress, she had seen enough to know that Rafe was a superior specimen of masculinity. The muscles of his broad shoulders and long arms looked exactly as if Michelangelo himself had sculpted them. His broad chest and firm stomach were likewise as chiseled in their musculature.

"So you know nothing at all about what will transpire between us this night?" Rafe asked.

Athena gulped as Rafe took her shoulders in his hands, turning her away from him. She held her breath a moment as she felt him begin unfastening the buttons at the back of her bodice.

"I-I know I am to share your bed," she managed to answer.

"Is that all you know?" he asked. His voice was low, deeper than was usual, and tinged with an intonation that caused Athena to feel as if someone were drizzling warm confection over her.

"Y-you might...you might kiss me?" she ventured.

Her body stiffened slightly as she felt Rafe's hands push her bodice from her shoulders—felt him loosen the laces of her corset and untie the band of her petticoat.

"I might," he mumbled.

Athena found that her knees went weak and feared she might faint away again—only this time with pleasure, for she felt Rafe press his lips to the bareness of her shoulder.

Slowly he pushed her bodice down until it settled at her waist. He gently stripped her corset from her— somewhat the way his mother had done when they'd put Athena to bed with exhaustion.

As Athena felt her petticoats and dress drop to the floor around her ankles, Rafe pressed his mouth to her ear, even as his hands lingered on her shoulders. "Step out of your clothes, Athena," he instructed in a voice so provocative, it caused goose pimples to race over Athena's arms and legs. "And turn and face me," he added.

Summoning every thread of courage she could, Athena stepped out of her clothing and—wearing only her camisole, pantaloons, and stockings—turned to face her husband.

She found, however, that she could not look up at Rafe. Her ignorance about what he expected from her, coupled with her fear and anxieties because of her naiveté, found her with no bravery.

Athena closed her eyes to shut out the shocking yet amiable sight of Rafe's bare chest before her. She felt him take her face in his hands, and when he raised her face upward and said, "Put your arms around me, Athena," she did find some strength somewhere inside her and did as he instructed.

The moment her hands touched the smooth warmth of his skin, Athena was astonished at her own reaction—her own desire to completely embrace him. And so she did. Slowly—for she was a bashful bride, after all—Athena slid her arms around Rafe's waist.

"Look at me, Athena," he said then. "Just open your eyes and look at me."

Gulping to try and quiet the mad pounding in her bosom—the ringing in her ears—Athena opened her eyes. Instantly she was mesmerized by Rafe's alluring gaze—by the pure comeliness of his face. Though she did not understand why, Athena felt a sudden slight surge of moisture flood her mouth—found herself staring at Rafe's lips for a moment, wanting to know what they would feel like pressed to her own.

Slowly, his hands slid from her face to gently encircle her neck, and Athena held her breath as Rafe's head descended toward hers—as he pressed his lips to hers in a tender kiss. He kissed her again, this time allowing his lips to linger to hers for a longer moment. Again he kissed her, and swirls of color began to spin in Athena's mind. Over and over Rafe kissed her, creating a sort of rhythm that inspired Athena to courage, and all at once, she realized she was kissing him back—melted against his firm, warm body and kissing him as fully as he was kissing her.

Suddenly, Athena had the sense that something inside her—something that had been pinned up or imprisoned until that moment—was liberated, set free, and she tightened her embrace of his waist as he kissed her again and again and again.

Abruptly it seemed, Rafe stepped back from her a ways. Taking her face in his hands once more, he gazed down into her eyes and asked, "Was that endurable?"

Blushing, for she was somewhat shy that she had divined so much pleasure from kissing him, she nodded. "Of course," she admitted in a whisper.

"Good," Rafe said.

He was smiling at her when she looked up to him again and asked, "So now we have consummated our marriage?" she asked.

Rafe's smile broadened, and he released her, stepping back from her. Striding to her wardrobe—the one his mother had stocked with beautiful dresses and fine undergarments—he opened the doors, choosing a nightgown and tossing it to the bed.

"Your innocence is attractive, you know," he said.

"So there's more to it than a kiss?" Athena asked.

Rafe still smiled, exhaling a heavy sigh. "Well, I would hope you would at least share my bed, Athena...sleep with me in it."

Athena smiled and giggled a little. "Oh, I promise you that after sleeping with my sisters—all four of us in a bed much smaller than yours is—I'm certain I can manage that."

Rafe chuckled, and Athena quickly slipped on her nightdress, even as Rafe stripped off his trousers to be clothed only in his long under-trousers.

"As I said," he chuckled, "your innocence is very attractive, Athena."

Folding back the bed covers, Rafe gestured that Athena should lie in bed first. Nervously, she lay down—yet attempting to lie as close to the edge of one side of the bed as she could.

"It's quite overly warm in here tonight," she sighed as Rafe lay down next to her. "By the size of the fire in the hearth, one would think Charles expected that you and I should be sleeping in our nothing-at-alls tonight."

Again Rafe chuckled. Athena looked over to see him lying on his back with his hands tucked under his head and gazing up at the ceiling.

"One would think that, wouldn't one?" he said, smiling as if he cached some great secret. "Good night then, Athena."

"Good night, Rafe," Athena said in return.

She knew it would be hours before she would be able to fall asleep, hours before the sensation left on her lips by Rafe's kiss—the warm, delicious tingle of it—would finally dissipate enough for her to find slumber. Even then, she wondered if she would ever leave wakefulness—for having Rafe lying in the bed next to her was a pleasure she had not expected to experience. To know he was there—hear his breathing, know that no harm would befall her, for Rafe was there to protect her—it was a euphoric, blissful awareness indeed.

"Thank you, Rafe," Athena said softly.

"And for what are you thanking me exactly?" he asked in return.

"Why, for saving my sisters and myself from destitution, of course," she told him.

"Oh, of course," he said. She fancied he sounded rather disappointed as he said, "You're welcome, Athena."

There would be no bad dreams that night—no visions of poverty and hunger, no fear. As Athena slept in her marriage bed with her benevolent, very handsome husband—her husband who had kissed her as she never imagined a woman could be kissed— for the first time since her parents were lost, Athena slept the sleep of pure serenity.

# CHAPTER EIGHT

Though Athena was still somewhat uncomfortable lingering in the kitchen dressed in only her nightgown, robe, and slippers, Annabel had that morning explained to her that it was the Dandridge family habit. Therefore, with the exception of Rafe, who was already dressed for his day of business, Mrs. Dandridge and all four Monroe girls sat at the breakfast table, hair still braided from the night before and enjoying bread and jam as the sun shone through frosted window panes.

"You will be home for supper then, Rafe?" Mrs. Dandridge asked.

"Of course, Mother," Rafe assured his mother. He looked to Athena then, smiled, and said, "You see there, Athena? You see how she told me I would be home for supper…even though it sounded like a question?"

Athena blushed as she returned Rafe's smile, nodding with understanding. Oh, Athena tried not to blush each time her gaze met Rafe's bronze eyes, but she'd found that after the moments of affection they'd exchanged the night before—the kisses they'd shared before retiring to bed—she could not look at him without her cheeks pinking up like summer roses. He was so heroic, after all—so dashing in his rescue of Athena and her sisters, so handsome. But it was more than that—something she'd sensed the night before when her head had finally been clear to think for the first time in ever so long. Ever since Rafe had kissed her—caressing her shoulders, her face, her neck—ever since the moment their lips had met, it was as if she'd had a glimpse of his soul. Furthermore, all during the night, whenever Athena would wake to find that she hadn't been dreaming of him, that he truly was lying next to her in their bed, she'd begun to remember things from the past— things about Rafe.

Certainly there was her most uncomfortable memory of him—the day he'd happened upon her and Fenton as Fenton had been about to kiss her. But that memory was pushed aside as others came flooding back. She remembered that Rafe had always been honorable, a gentleman, kind and charitable, respectful of anyone no matter their class or situation. Even as a very young man, a boy, he had ever been the same. Athena likewise began to think back on the evening that she and her sisters had come caroling to the Dandridges'. In her mind, she could see Rafe's face as he stood in the parlor watching his mother converse with them, and Athena realized that it must've been those moments when Rafe decided to sacrifice his freedom to choose a bride from an undoubtedly endless list of women—to sacrifice a great deal of his financial security as well—all to help her and her sisters and return honor to the name he felt his father had tarnished. The realization had astonished Athena, in truth. For indeed she and her sisters had not lingered more than half the hour in Mrs. Dandridge's parlor. It was a quick determination by a powerful man. Additionally, there was the fact that Rafe had arrived on their Camden Town stoop before sunrise the next morning. How had he found them so quickly? she had wondered. And then she remembered Rafe's whispering to Charles that same night and surmised Rafe must've sent Charles to follow them once they'd left the Dandridge house.

It was a great deal to take in—the broad spectrum of Rafe's decision, planning, and self-sacrifice. And though Athena had known she would grow to love Rafe for his heroism and goodness, if nothing else, she had been quite astonished to awaken that morning to find that she already did love him for it. Moreover, she was *in* love with him—and not just for the sake of his deliverance of her and her sisters from their misery.

As Athena had lain in bed next to Rafe that morning before he'd awakened—as memories of the boy he'd been and the young man he grew into returned to her—she realized that she'd always carried a deep fondness, infatuation, and admiration for Rafe Dandridge. Yet she likewise knew why it had been Fenton that had distracted her—and one day stolen a kiss from her. It was for the mere fact that Fenton tried! Fenton was flirtatious, flattering, gregarious, and charming—charming in a different way than his elder brother. Athena realized that Fenton had pursued her when she was a girl just younger than Annabel was now, and it had been flattering to her. And the flattering attention from

Rafe's younger brother had made Fenton seem more obtainable than Rafe. Youth, naiveté, and simple immaturity had found Athena's head turned from Rafe to Fenton. And when Fenton had kissed her and she'd discovered how unpleasant his kiss was—well, Rafe was away on his father's business, and so Athena had let go of the idea of capturing his attention in any way. After all, he was six years her senior, and her being only fourteen at the time—it would have been strange if she'd actually managed to arrest his attention then.

But now—now she was married to him! And her mind was free of the weight and worry and misery of trying to feed and shelter her sisters. For the past year, Athena had thought of nothing but survival. Yet now that her survival was assured, because of Rafe's championing them, her mind felt fresh and alive and able to reason in a way it hadn't been able to since her father's ruination and death. She could see clearly that, somehow, God had managed to gift her the one thing she'd wanted since she was a young girl: Rafe Dandridge.

"And did you get a case of the bashful bride last night, Athena?" Marta asked, startling Athena from her reverie.

"What?" Athena stammered, feeling a fresh blush rise to her cheeks.

"Your big sister was quite comfortable sharing my bed, I think, Marta," Rafe said, grinning at Athena and causing her blush to deepen.

"Really?" Mrs. Dandridge asked, her smile broadening to the length of the Nile.

"Well, that's because she's used to sleeping with all three of us," Marta explained. "And now she only has to sleep with you, Rafe."

"So…you fared well last night, Athena?" Mrs. Dandridge asked, her lovely eyes wide with joy and curiosity.

"Oh…oh yes, mum," Athena stammered. "I slept quite peacefully."

"Although it was somewhat too warm in our bedchamber, Mother," Rafe said, staring at his mother with suspicion. "In fact, it was so overly warm that Athena remarked to me that perhaps Charles thought we meant to sleep in our nothing-at-alls."

"Too warm, was it?" Mrs. Dandridge asked—and Athena thought the woman looked a bit mischievously guilty. "Well, I'll make certain to mention to Charles that he should light a lesser fire in your chamber tonight."

"Please do," Rafe said. He winked at his mother, adding, "There will be nights enough for warmer fires, eventually…I am sure."

"Are you really going to contact the headmistress of Prominence, Rafe?" Annabel suddenly asked.

Rafe nodded to her, smiled, and said, "I'll send word to her today, Annabel. Not to worry. It may take some time for the correspondence, but I'm sure you will be packed up and off to Prominence within a fortnight."

Annabel squealed with delight, clapping her hands with anticipation.

"And may we be excused, Rafe?" Marta inquired. "Bronwen and I have a full day of dollhouse planned…if you don't mind too much."

"Of course you may be excused, Marta," Rafe said, smiling at Marta and then Bronwen. "My, my, but you Monroe girls are well-mannered," he chuckled.

"I'll come with you, girls," Annabel said, "if I may be excused as well, Rafe."

"Of course," Rafe chuckled. Placing his napkin on the table beside his plate, he stood as the girls scampered off toward the parlor.

"I'm off as well, ladies," he said. "You both enjoy your day." Looking to Athena, he added, "And *you* should take some extra rest. Exhaustion lingers if one's not careful."

Athena smiled at him, grateful for his concern. "Very well."

Mrs. Dandridge leaned toward Athena then, whispering, "And remind him that he *will* be home for supper."

Amused, Athena giggled a little as she said, "And you will be home for supper, Rafe?"

Rafe laughed and kissed the top of Athena's head and then the top of his mother's, saying, "Trying to teach my wife your tricks already, eh, Mother?"

Mrs. Dandridge shrugged with feigning ignorance, and Rafe strode from the room. The moment he was gone, Athena experienced a sense of insecurity.

Suddenly Mrs. Dandridge took her hand and, smiling at her with eyes as wide as dinner plates, asked, "Well? Did everything proceed well last night, darling?"

"I-I'm not sure to what you are referring, Mrs. Dandridge," Athena stammered. She was a little taken aback by the woman's prying question. Not angry with her—just taken aback.

"I mean, is my son a good lover to you?" Mrs. Dandridge asked. "Did he treat you with respect as he should? Did he please you?"

Blushing to her toes, Athena answered, "I-I...I don't know how to respond, in truth, Mrs. Dandridge. Rafe...he was very kind to me. He...he was very kind."

Mrs. Dandridge frowned. She inhaled a deep breath and exhaled slowly. "You do own an understanding of the marital relations between a husband and wife, don't you, Athena?"

Athena shrugged, however. "I'm not really certain, to be honest, Mrs. Dandridge." As Athena's brows puckered with curiosity, she lowered her voice and admitted, "I do feel as if I am somewhat uninformed on the subject. But I'm sure the comprehension will be mine, sooner or later."

Mrs. Dandridge bit her lower lip, as if she wanted to say something but was doubtful she should say it. At last, she simply said, "I suppose so, dear."

They heard a knock on the front door then.

"I'll see to it, mum!" Annabel called from the parlor.

"No, Annabel!" Athena called in return. "You're not even dressed!"

But it was too late—and the moment Athena heard Fenton's voice greet Annabel, she knew exactly why her sister had been so quick to answer the door.

"It's Fenton come to visit us, Mrs. Dandridge!" Annabel called.

A moment later, Fenton stepped into the kitchen, dressed up like a dandy and with Annabel at his heels like a spaniel.

"Good morning, ladies!" Fenton greeted. Going to his mother, he kissed her cheek. Then turning to look at Athena, he said, "And I see the new Mrs. Dandridge is quite recovered and looking as beautiful as ever. How splendid for Rafe, hmmm?"

"You know we breakfast at this hour, Fenton," Mrs. Dandridge softly scolded. "You'll have to curtail your spontaneity now that we have young ladies living here. It's not proper for you to see them so casually dressed. Especially Rafe's wife."

"Ah yes," Fenton said, staring at Athena with obvious wanton desire. "Rafe's wife. And to think, Athena, that you and I once—"

"I may be leaving soon, Fenton," Annabel interrupted—and Athena was thankful that she did.

"Really, love?" Fenton asked, though he continued to stare at Athena a moment before looking to Annabel. "And why so? Has your tyrant of a brother-in-law severed your patience already?"

"No, of course not," Annabel answered. Straightening her posture proudly, she told him, "I'm going to attend Prominence. Rafe says they may accept me within a fortnight."

"Well!" Fenton exclaimed. "I thought sure you were too old to attend Prominence, for you are already such a polished young lady."

Annabel giggled with delight at Fenton's flattery, and Athena felt sick in her stomach, for she could see her younger self in Annabel's gullibility then—and her heart ached for her sister.

"I think it's time we all of us got dressed," Mrs. Dandridge said, rising from her chair. "Here, Fenton. Have some breakfast while we girls ready for the day. We should be back promptly."

"Very well," Fenton said, settling in a chair at the table. "Be about your toilette. I shall be here when you return."

"Come along, Annabel," Mrs. Dandridge said, taking Annabel's hand. "Marta, Bronwen, time to get dressed, darlings."

As Annabel followed Mrs. Dandridge to her chambers, scowling all the way with disappointment at having to leave Fenton, Athena stood, saying, "Excuse me, Fenton. We'll all return shortly."

But she gasped when she felt Fenton take hold of her wrist. "Just a moment there, little Miss Athena," he said, frowning at her.

Marta and Bronwen scurried past them on their way to their bedchamber, and when they'd gone, Fenton stood, pulling Athena with him into the parlor.

"You act so indifferent to me, Athena," Fenton said in an angry whisper. "As if nothing has ever passed between us."

Gulping with distress, Athena said, "Nothing ever passed between us, Fenton."

"Didn't it?" he asked, his eyes narrowing. "Don't you remember our kiss, Athena? That day in the orchards?" One of his hands grasped her throat, and he said, "Perhaps I should kiss you again. Perhaps then you'll remember."

"I am your brother's wife, Fenton," Athena firmly reminded him. "Let go of me."

But Fenton did not let go of her—only smiled with a malice that caused her to begin to tremble with trepidation.

"My brother's wife," he mumbled. "Yes… Annabel has told me all about how you came to be my brother's wife. But I know your secret, Athena. I know that it was always me you wanted." He lowered his voice, pressed his lips to her ear, and said, "And you still want me, don't you?" He laughed in his throat, adding, "You know Rafe will never be the man I am."

"You're right, Fenton," Athena said. "Rafe could never be the likes of you. Now let me go before I scream and your mother finds out how truly despicable you are."

But Fenton clamped his free hand over Athena's mouth, pushing her back against the wall as he growled, "You'll not say a word against me to my family, Athena. Not to Rafe and certainly not to my mother. For if you do, I *will* tell Rafe about you and me—about our kiss in the orchard those years ago…the one he did not manage to interrupt. And you don't want your hero to know that I had you first, do you? You don't want Rafe to know what a miserable little trollop he rescued from Camden Town, eh? What would he think of you then, if he knew I had you first? Do you think he would still take such pity on you? Pay for your insipid sister's schooling? You know he wouldn't. You know how he feels about me. You would disgust him if he knew I'd tasted your kiss long before he did."

Tears escaped Athena's eyes to travel over her cheeks.

"Oh, don't cry, pretty Athena," Fenton said, releasing her then. "Our secret is safe with me...for now." He stepped back from her, smiling a triumphant smile as he studied her from head to toe a moment. "Now run along...before Rafe returns and finds you flaunting yourself before me thus."

"Stay away from my sister," Athena growled through her tears.

But Fenton only smiled. "Are you willing to take her place in my affections?"

"Stay away from her, or I'll tell Rafe myself about that horrid day in the orchard...no matter the consequences."

Fenton chuckled with amusement. "No, you won't." Then taking her arm and turning her toward the stairs, Fenton slapped Athena on the seat and said, "Now run along, Mrs. Dandridge. You're not properly dressed to receive company."

Fleeing from him as fast as her feet would carry her, Athena raced into the bedchamber she now shared with Rafe, closing the door behind her and bolting it.

Burying her face in her hands, Athena tried to calm herself. She could not melt from exhaustion again—nor from fear of Fenton revealing what he knew to Rafe. She had to be strong, just as she'd had to carry on when her mother had died—when her father had lost everything and then followed her mother to heaven. It was the same depth of strength Athena needed to find once more. Yes, Rafe had saved her—plucked Athena and her sisters from certain continued misery and perhaps worse. Therefore, she would not embarrass him or evoke his disgust toward her by revealing what she'd done as a naive girl when she'd let Fenton kiss her in the orchard years before. She would simply have to be strong, to put off Fenton at every turn, and she would certainly need to see Annabel off to Prominence posthaste!

Gathering more strength of determination as she dressed, Athena straightened her posture and eventually returned downstairs. There she found Annabel sitting on the sofa with Fenton—Mrs. Dandridge sitting in a chair across the room, staring at Fenton with an expression of mingled disappointment and warning.

Athena knew then that her happiness was simply not meant to be. It would be spoiled whether or not Rafe would one day return the feelings she already had for him—the growing, near obsessive love swelling in her heart for her champion. Her happiness had been spoiled with Fenton's appearance. Yet unhappiness was not physical misery, and Athena thought she could endure her own unhappiness for the safety, welfare, and happiness of her sisters; she could endure it for the sake of Rafe's honor and pride. She could. She must.

# CHAPTER NINE

"She's been very pale ever since Fenton arrived this morning," Florence whispered to her eldest son. "I fear he may have said something hurtful to her."

Rafe frowned, angry with his brother. "But what could he have said?" he asked his mother.

Florence shook her head, however, answering, "I don't know. But I saw a noticeable change in her, Rafe." As her eyes brimmed with tears, she choked, "You're going to have to tell him he's not welcome in your home, Rafe. Now that the girls are here—now that you have Athena to protect and care for—Fenton cannot be coming in and out at will and upsetting my new daughters and your wife."

"He's your son, Mother," Rafe said. In truth, he was relieved to hear his mother suggest he put Fenton away from them all. His brother seemed to have misery to others sewn to his boot heel. But he'd never caused any true pain to his mother or Rafe before. Still, as Rafe peeked around the corner to see Athena sitting at the kitchen table, wringing her hands with anxiety, Rafe could see the worry, the weight of something unpleasant in her countenance.

When he'd left her that morning at breakfast, Athena's cheeks had been rosy, her smile easy and full of tranquility. But now—now she looked nearly as burden-laden as she had the night she and her sisters had happened upon his stoop while caroling.

"I was in the livery for some time today, Mother," Rafe said. "Let me bathe quickly, and then I will see if Athena will confide in me, all right?"

"All right, darling," Florence agreed. "But hurry, won't you? Fenton said he was planning on returning for supper with us."

"I can promise you this, Mother," Rafe growled. "If Fenton is in any way the cause of Athena's distress...he will never be dining with us in my house again."

"I understand, Rafe," Florence agreed, brushing a tear from her cheek. "I do. And I support your decision to tell him so."

"Very well," Rafe said, exhaling a heavy breath. "A quick bath and I will be back down. All right?"

Florence nodded, and he could see her worry. Kissing her forehead, he assured her, "All will be well, Mother. I did not marry the girl simply to change her venue of despair."

"I know, darling," Florence said.

But as Rafe turned, intending to ascend the stairs, his mother caught his arm, stalling him.

"There is one thing more, Rafe," she said.

"Yes?" Rafe asked.

Glancing about to first ensure their privacy, his mother whispered, "I do not think Athena has any knowledge whatsoever about a woman and her marital responsibilities to her husband where…where intimate goings-on are concerned."

Rafe smiled, nodded, and said, "Oh, I am quite sure you are right, Mother." He chuckled, adding, "But don't worry. I am no wanton ogre of carnal demand. And nature will find its course…eventually."

"I know," Florence said. "And thank you, darling, for being such a good, honorable man. You are my only pride and my greatest joy."

"Thank you, Mother," Rafe said. He placed another kiss to the top of his mother's head and then ascended the stairs three at a time.

His fury with his brother was fully provoked—for he knew, without doubt, that Athena's expression of panic and despair was Fenton's doing, somehow. Quickly, he filled the copper tub in his bedchamber with the cauldron of water Charles had put to heat on the fire. Adding the cold water from the pitcher on the washbasin table, he stripped off his clothes and prepared to bathe hastily.

The manner in which Athena had looked at him that morning as she sat across from him at the breakfast table—it had instilled hope in Rafe, hope that she could care for him one day. The fact was, Rafe had been taken aback at how quickly he'd begun to adore Athena again. When he'd first thought of offering her himself and all he had in order to somewhat offset the misery his father had caused her and her family, Rafe thought it was because of his own feelings of guilt. But he'd quickly realized that the fondness he'd secreted for the girl several years before had begun anew the moment he'd seen her standing in the parlor with her sisters that cold winter's night.

When Athena had been first infatuated with Fenton, she had been just a girl of fourteen. But by the time she was sixteen, she'd unknowingly managed to capture Rafe's interest and attention—managed to commence in capturing his heart. Yet when he'd returned from conducting business for her father abroad two years later, it was to learn of the Monroe family's inconceivable tragedies and to find Athena Monroe had vanished. Rafe had sent out many inquiries, but no one knew where the Monroe girls had gone, and he had reconciled himself to never seeing her again.

And then as fate would have it, she appeared— and in great need of assistance—assistance that Rafe was fortunately able to provide. He'd managed to gather Athena and her sisters under his roof, to marry Athena. But to what end? If Fenton had already upset Athena—or worse, rekindled her infatuation with him—everyone's happiness was at risk—not just Athena's, not just his. Therefore, whether Athena had once owned feelings for Fenton—whether she even still thought she currently owned feelings for him—

Fenton would ruin her if he had the chance. Thus, Rafe would not give him the chance. If presented with a choice between his wife and his brother—the choice was not a difficult one to make. Fenton would have to be dealt with.

Athena heard Annabel answer the door—heard Fenton's voice in response to her sister's greeting. Oh, how she wished Rafe had returned from his day's business! How she longed to have him take her hand and place it in the crook of his arm, letting her know that he would protect her and that all would be well.

All the day long—since the moment Fenton had finally taken his leave that morning—Athena has struggled over what course she should take. Fenton had threatened her—treated her very inappropriately. Yet if she told Rafe of what had transpired, would he believe her? Even if he did, what if Fenton kept his word—followed through with his threat to tell Rafe of the dalliance she and Fenton had had in the orchard so many years ago? What then? Would Rafe annul their marriage? Send Athena and her sisters back to Camden Town and destitution?

In her heart, Athena knew Rafe would not forsake her. He had pledged himself to care for her—for

Annabel, Marta, and Bronwen. But she feared that, should Fenton reveal the past, Rafe might not treat her with quite so much tenderness—might not bless her with the delicious affections of his kiss and caress the way he had the previous night. And being that Athena's heart had always been drawn to Rafe Dandridge, she could not bear the thought of him harboring any sort of contempt for her.

Thus, Athena knew not what to do, and it had worn her to the core with worry all the day long. And now Fenton had returned—to mock her, no doubt. Athena imagined the horror of them all sitting down to sup together—imagined Fenton flirting with Annabel, simply to frighten Athena. Imagined, even worse, that he might flirt with *her* and raise Rafe's suspicions—and she could not face Fenton in that moment.

Therefore, before Annabel had the opportunity to bring him into the kitchen where Athena sat, she fled, hurrying up the stairs, even as she heard Mrs. Dandridge greet her younger son in the parlor.

Racing up the stairs to the bedchamber she now shared with Rafe—her husband, her every dream come true in a man—Athena flung open the door, fairly leaping into the room and then turning to slam the door closed behind her.

Her head was pounding so hard from her anxiety as well as sprinting up the stairs that she leaned her head against the door a moment in order to catch her breath.

"Athena? Are you all right?" she heard Rafe ask from behind her.

Whirling around, Athena gasped when she saw Rafe standing near the bed, with only a towel wrapped around his waist for modesty—his hair near dripping wet.

"I'm so sorry, Rafe!" she exclaimed, covering her eyes with her hands at once. "I-I did not know you had returned home. I'm sorry!"

Turning to face the door once more, Athena kept one hand over her eyes as she fumbled with the door latch in trying to open it.

"Wait," Rafe said.

She heard him striding toward her—felt his warm hands on her shoulders as he said, "What's the matter, Athena? You look like you've been seeing spirits roaming about the hallways. You're positively pale, love."

All at once, Athena turned to face him again. "What did you say to me?" she asked in a whisper.

Rafe, though frowning with concern, grinned a little and asked, "Are you all right? Has something...or someone upset you?"

Athena would've thought it impossible, but the truth of it was Rafe was even more attractive with his hair wet and tousled and standing before her in such a vulnerable state of undress. All at once she saw him as more approachable than intimidating—and the change in her view of him prompted her courage.

"Fenton is here, Rafe," she said in a whisper. "And...and he was here earlier today. And when he was here, he...he...he threatened to tell you something about me—something about me...and something about him...something that happened years and years ago when I was..."

Athena gasped, startled out of her confession by a knock on the door and Fenton's voice beyond it, calling, "Are you in there, Athena? I saw you trying to hide from me. Shall I let myself in?"

"Rafe, I..." Athena began as tears began streaming down her face.

"It's all right, Athena," Rafe said, taking her face between his hands and smiling at her. "Nothing you could tell me could change my heart where you're concerned." He kissed her tenderly on the lips and then whispered, "Now step aside, please." His smile broadened as he added, "And you may want to turn your back to me a moment."

"Why?" Athena asked.

Rafe took hold of her shoulders, moving her away from the door.

Fenton knocked again, saying, "I know you're in there, Athena. Come now, and let your old lover in for a bit."

And as Rafe began to loose the towel from about his waist, Athena understood his intention—at least somewhat—and turned from him. She heard the door open and held her breath.

"Fenton," Rafe began, "why are you knocking on my bedchamber door inquiring after my wife?"

There was a pause—such a long pause, in fact, that Athena thought that perhaps Rafe had stepped out of the room, even for the state of his entire undress. But when she started to look behind her and caught sight of his towel discarded on the floor, his bare feet and legs nearby, she quickly abandoned her intent to see whether Rafe were still with her—for it was obvious that he was.

"I…I thought perhaps…I thought I had upset her somehow and came to offer my apologies," Fenton stammered.

"Well, Fenton, Athena is in fact here with me now," Rafe said. "But we are privately engaged, and you will have to offer any apologies owed to her at some future time. Also, please inform Mother that Athena and I will not be down for supper tonight. At least not for the time being."

"Very well," Fenton growled. "But there is something you should know about Athena, Rafe," he began.

Terrified that Fenton might tell Rafe the truth of their kiss in the orchard before she had a chance to confess it, Athena spun around, careless of Rafe's state of undress.

"Rafe, I…" she began. But the awe of seeing Rafe's backside without his towel about him stunned her into silence as well as covering her eyes once more.

"Fenton," Rafe began, "Athena has told me everything. And the fact that you think such adolescent flirtations would intimidate me into worrying that Athena might favor you over me is…well, it's laughable, Fenton. So go down to supper with Mother, and know this: it is the last time you will dine in my home, with my family. And if I ever again hear of you attempting to unsettle my wife, even just a little, or speaking ill of her to anyone or in any way…I promise that I will crush your dandy of a head between my hands. Do you understand me, little brother?"

"You don't deserve her," Fenton growled.

"Of course not," Rafe said. "But you do not deserve to even look at her. Now be gone, Fenton. And hopefully, one day, when you've come to your senses, we can be brothers once more. But until then, stay out of my way and away from my wife."

Athena heard Rafe slam the door and draw the bolt. Yet she did not drop her hands from her already closed eyes until he chuckled, "It's all right, love. I've wrapped the towel around myself and am once again modest."

"I don't know if your mother would consider wearing only a towel as proper modesty," Athena said, still covering her eyes.

"Well, you're not my mother, are you?" Rafe chuckled. She felt him take hold of her hand then, pushing it from her face. "Now tell me…what is this awful secret between you and Fenton that he was holding over you?"

Opening her eyes, Athena gazed up into Rafe's handsome, compassionate face. "Years ago, when I was fourteen, he…he kissed me…in your mother's orchard."

"Did he now?" Rafe asked, grinning.

"Yes…and I promise it was the most repulsive experience I had ever had, Rafe! I promise," Athena babbled desperately. "It was vile, Rafe. Nothing like the way you kissed me last night! It made me feel sick for a week!"

"And when I kissed you last night?" Rafe asked.

"Well, that I could've lingered in doing for hours," Athena shyly admitted. "But Fenton said you would loathe me for having kissed him! He said you wouldn't—"

"Shhh," Rafe whispered, placing his fingers to her lips. "Fenton holds nothing over you, Athena. And he certainly holds nothing over me." He chuckled to himself a moment and then added, "You know that I was fascinated by you before I left to go abroad for my father's business, don't you?"

Athena frowned. Surely he was only teasing her. "You don't have to pretend that you—"

"I'm not pretending, Athena," Rafe said. "I even made many inquiries as to what had become of you when I returned home to find you and your sisters had vanished after your father's death. But no one knew where you were." He smiled, brushed a strand of hair from her cheek, and continued, "And then you were there—standing in my parlor, sitting on my sofa, drinking my mother's wassail, and eating her Christmas biscuits."

Athena's heart began to swell as she understood that he was, indeed, telling her the truth. She could see the truth in the smoldering bronze of his eyes.

"And you sent Charles to follow us, didn't you?" she asked.

"I did," he admitted.

"I watched you from afar...all my life," Athena confessed. "But I always knew I was born too late for you to take notice of me...to care for me...to..."

Rafe's arms were around her then, holding her firm against his warm, strong body as his mouth captured hers in a kiss of such heated, passionate hunger that it left her limp and helpless in his arms for a time. All at once, such powerful feelings of desire—such potent sensations of rapture and bliss—

washed over Athena that she thought sure she would burst into a thousand radiant pieces of illumination!

Over and over Rafe kissed her, and each time Athena welcomed the demands of his mouth—met and matched the rhythm of his affections. She was being carried away to she didn't know what—but she knew she did not want to resist whatever it was.

Suddenly, however, Rafe released her, and she stumbled backward several steps.

She watched as he raked his hands back through his hair, combing it with his fingers in obvious frustration.

"Do I...do I disappoint you, Rafe?" she ventured, fearful of his answer.

He frowned at her, however, shaking his head and assuring her, "No, never. It's just that...well, there is more to men than you comprehend, Athena."

Athena smiled, all at once amused by the realization of her own naiveté where men were concerned.

"Oh, that I wholeheartedly admit," she said to him. She was dizzy—nearly intoxicated by the lingering euphoria he'd showered her in. "I mean, women never stand unclothed in front of one another...even sisters. But men—obviously, you and

151

Fenton are not such strangers to nakedness as…as some of us are."

Rafe smiled, strode to their bed, and sat down, shaking his head as he too laughed a little. "It was something I read in my studies at school, years and years ago," he began, "about certain native tribes in North America—tribes whose warriors stand naked before their enemies to convey their own lack of fear. The thought came to me when Fenton arrived. He's a conceited twit, Athena, but I've always bested him…at everything. Yet I admit to being somewhat concerned that you might, in fact, still find him more, shall we say, interesting than I. And so in viewing him as my enemy—my competitor for your affections—I remembered the native tribes of North America and their means of intimidation by standing naked before their enemies." He looked over at her and smiled. "And it would seem that it's a very effective form of intimidation, indeed."

Athena laughed and sat down next to him on the bed. "So it would seem."

"I wish you could have seen the expression of pure shock on Fenton's face," Rafe laughed. He stood, raking his hands through his hair again—only this time he seemed far more at ease about it.

"Rafe," Athena began.

"Yes?" Rafe asked.

Though Athena was frightened concerning what she did not know in relation to what transpired between husband and wife in private, she was also curious and wanting to be a wife that pleased her husband in every regard.

And so she continued, "I know you did not tell me everything about husbands and wives last night. Will you tell me now?"

Athena smiled, for she was certain Rafe was blushing.

"You are sweet, Athena—so kind and self-sacrificing…and innocent in yet many ways, even for all that you have endured," he said. "I pause in…in telling you…"

"Then show me," Athena ventured. "If I tell you…if I confess to you that I have wanted you for my own always, secretly, as far back as I can remember and that I woke from my sleep of exhaustion to knowing I had somehow, in a mere matter of hours, fallen assuredly in love with you— that I want nothing more than to be your wife and love you with all my heart—then will you confide in me all that I do not know about loving you?"

Rafe leaned toward her, placing his fisted hands on either side of her on the bed and gazing into her eyes. Being that Athena was looking up at him, her head tilted backward, Rafe bent, placing a soft, moist, and lingering kiss to her throat. Caressing her throat with another kiss as his mouth moved up her neck, to her chin, and then to press a hunger-driven kiss to her mouth, Rafe then said, "I could never deny you anything, Athena. And I fell in love with you the instant you told the vicar that you took me to be your husband and then fainted in my arms." He kissed her again, longingly—fiercely. "You have long been the object of my affection, of my love, and now you are the object of my ravenous desire as well. So yes, I will confide in you all that I know about our loving one another that you do not. But I would prefer to show you, rather than speak it."

"Very well, Rafe," Athena said, reaching up to hold his handsome face between her hands. "Will there be more kissing then?" she asked playfully.

"Oh, indeed," Rafe answered, pressing a kiss to her mouth. "Much more kissing."

"Oh, good! I am very glad of that," Athena whispered. "I do *so* like the way you kiss me, Rafe." She giggled as he again placed a long, moist kiss to her throat. "Though I am a bit worried that your towel might loosen and fall away at some point."

Rafe simply laughed, laid Athena back on their bed, and, as he covered her body with his own, said, "Don't worry about that now, love. Don't worry about anything at all. Just let me love you."

# EPILOGUE

"Why are you blushing, Athena?" Marta asked as everyone in the Dandridge house sat together at breakfast the next morning.

"Whatever do you mean, Marta?" Athena asked, feigning ignorance—though she knew exactly to what Marta was referring. She did blush every time she looked at her handsome husband—at her lover, who had loved her all the night long.

"Every time you look to Rafe, or he to you, you blush, Athena," Marta pointed out.

"Well, I'm sure it's just because my son is so handsome, Marta," Mrs. Dandridge intervened.

"And why isn't Rafe dressed for going out yet today?" Marta next inquired.

Rafe shrugged, winked at Athena, and answered, "I decided to have a day at home with my new family. It is my prerogative, you know, Marta."

"But you didn't even comb your hair, Rafe!" Marta noted. "You look like you slept terribly fitful last night, with your hair all tousled like that."

"Forgive me my slovenly appearance, little sister," Rafe chuckled. "I'll do better tomorrow, all right?"

Marta shrugged with indifference and drizzled honey on her porridge.

"That reminds me, Rafe," Mrs. Dandridge began, "I've found a house I'd like you to help me purchase."

"What?" Athena heard Rafe exclaim in unison with herself.

"Whatever would you need a house for, Mother?" he asked. "You live here."

"Well, it's just four doors down the row, and I've been thinking that I might like to have my own space again—somewhere where my little Marta and Bronwen can keep me company when Annabel goes to school."

"But this is your home, mum," Athena offered.

Mrs. Dandridge smiled at Athena, saying, "When will you ever start calling me Mother, Athena darling?

All of you girls, for that matter? I would so enjoy it if you called me Mother."

Athena smiled, her heart even more tender toward Mrs. Dandridge.

"Very well. But this is your home, Mother," Athena said.

"I know," Mrs. Dandridge said. "But I just feel as if I want my own space again. And I was hoping Marta and Bronwen would come live with me. After all, I have nothing to fill my time, and I do so love doting on the girls. You too, Annabel."

"Well, with my leaving for Prominence soon, I couldn't stay very long, Mrs. Dandr…Mother," Annabel said. Then smiling, she added, "But I would love to live with you for as long as possible, and of course when I come home for holidays."

"Mother," Rafe began, "there's no reason for you to—"

"I've made up my mind, darling," Mrs. Dandridge interrupted, however. "So if you don't wish to help me with the purchase, I'll simply call upon our solicitor."

Rafe exhaled a sigh of understanding. "Very well, Mother. I'll see to the purchase for you…today, if you like."

"Wonderful!" Mrs. Dandridge exclaimed. Then, rising from her chair, she said, "Now, girls—Annabel, Marta, Bronwen—let's get dressed. I want you three to visit the shoppes with me today."

"But what about Athena?" Bronwen asked. "Shouldn't she come with us? What will she do home all alone?"

"Oh, I think Rafe can manage to amuse Athena today," Mrs. Dandridge said, winking at her son.

Athena smiled as Rafe commented, "Yes, it's about time Athena and I had a go at that new dollhouse Father Christmas brought. The Noah's ark as well."

"Marvelous idea!" Mrs. Dandridge exclaimed. "Now, come along, girls. Let's get going."

Once Mrs. Dandridge and the girls had left the kitchen to ready in their rooms, Rafe fairly leapt from his chair and pulled Athena from hers and into his arms, claiming her mouth with his own.

"What *would* you like to do with me today, Mrs. Dandridge?" he asked. "A stroll in the park? The Noah's ark?"

Athena smiled up at him. "Is kissing you all the day long an option?" she asked.

"Of course," Rafe breathed, kissing her again.

"Then I choose that. I want to kiss you all the day long," Athena breathed.

Their lips met in a loving kiss for a moment, and then Rafe pulled away to look at her for a moment.

"I think that my mother is making plans for us—plans so that we can kiss all the day long every day if we wish," he said.

Athena's heart swelled with tender, thankful feelings toward her thoughtful, self-sacrificing mother-in-law.

"Yes, so it would seem," Athena said. "She's a very loving, thoughtful woman. You are very fortunate to have her."

"Yes, I am," Rafe agreed. "And even more fortunate to have the object of my affection in my arms at last."

"I would have you keep me in your arms always, Rafe," Athena whispered.

"I would have you keep me in your heart always, love," Rafe mumbled against her mouth. "Always."

"Always, my love," Athena breathed as Rafe's mouth blended with her own, sealing so many as yet even unspoken promises that would end in, *Always, my love*.

# AUTHOR'S NOTE

I'm not going to mince words: I wrote this book for me—just for fun and just because I wanted to have a little taste of Christmas!

Now I realize that this novella is about as cliché as they come, but that was my intent. I love cliché romance! It makes me smile and feel satisfied. And even though this story could have, of course, been longer, I simply wanted to write a little treat for myself that I could share with friends. I can just see myself now, this coming December, snatching up some little tins of shortbread Christmas cookies and using my glittery wire ribbon to tie them up with a copy of this book as a little something friends can enjoy when their reading time may be short but their need to read and relax—to escape and enjoy—is perhaps stronger than ever!

Once in awhile, we all need to do something for ourselves. For me, it's writing something less stressful and just for fun! In fact, along those lines, I'll just include a few very quick snippets. After all, the idea of this story is for it to be a quick fix—not a long commitment, right?

Thanks for joining me for a little random, cliché, touch-of-Christmas romance today!

Love your nutty friend,
Marcia Lynn McClure

**Snippet #1**—I've always wanted a fancy, shmancy dollhouse! Ha ha, really! I pause, however, in getting one for two reasons. One, I really don't have anywhere to keep it. And two, I've seen way too many creepy movies and TV series episodes that involve dollhouses. Yikes!

**Snippet #2**—All throughout the writing of this story, I was craving those little shortbread cookies with the red and green granulated sugar sprinkled on them.

I'm *still* craving those, and they're months and months away! Ahhh!

**Snippet #3**—I named our hero Rafe…because Rafe is kind of a cliché romance novel hero name, you know? Plus, I like the name Rafe!

**Snippet #4**—I named Athena because ever since I was, like, thirteen or something and saw the *original* Battlestar Galactica television series, I've liked the name. I mean, it always bugged me that Starbuck (the hot, bad-boy character in the series) liked Cassiopeia instead of the girl who really loved him, Athena. I'm still not over that one. Grrr.

**Snippet #5**—That delicious neck kiss thing Rafe does to Athena? Yep! *Love* when Kevin does that to me. Ha ha, TMI for sure! Oh well! Sorry, Kev, but the world needs to know how *fabulous* you really are!

To the object of **MY** affection…
*My husband, Kevin!*

# ABOUT THE AUTHOR

Marcia Lynn McClure's intoxicating succession of novels, novellas, and e-books—including *A Crimson Frost*, *The Visions of Ransom Lake*, *Kissing Cousins* and *Weathered too Young*—has established her as one of the most favored and engaging authors of true romance. Her unprecedented forte in weaving captivating stories of western, medieval, regency, and contemporary amour void of brusque intimacy has earned her the title "The Queen of Kissing."

Marcia, who was born in Albuquerque, New Mexico, has spent her life intrigued with people, history, love, and romance. A wife, mother, grandmother, family historian, poet, and author, Marcia Lynn McClure spins her tales of splendor for the sake of offering respite through the beauty, mirth, and delight of a worthwhile and wonderful story.

# BIBLIOGRAPHY

A Bargained-For Bride

Beneath the Honeysuckle Vine

A Better Reason to Fall in Love

The Bewitching of Amoretta Ipswich

Born for Thorton's Sake

The Chimney Sweep Charm

Christmas Kisses

A Crimson Frost

Daydreams

Desert Fire

Divine Deception

Dusty Britches

The Fragrance of her Name

A Good-Lookin' Man

The Haunting of Autumn Lake

The Heavenly Surrender

The Highwayman of Tanglewood

Kiss in the Dark

Kissing Cousins

The Light of the Lovers' Moon

Love Me

The Man of Her Dreams

The McCall Trilogy

Midnight Masquerade

The Object of His Affection
An Old-Fashioned Romance
One Classic Latin Lover, Please
The Pirate Ruse
The Prairie Prince
The Rogue Knight
Romance at the Christmas Tree Lot
The Romancing of Evangeline Ipswich
Romantic Vignettes
Saphyre Snow
Shackles of Honor
The Secret Bliss of Calliope Ipswich
Sudden Storms
Sweet Cherry Ray
Take a Walk With Me
The Tide of the Mermaid Tears
The Time of Aspen Falls
To Echo the Past
The Touch of Sage
The Trove of the Passion Room
Untethered
The Visions of Ransom Lake
Weathered Too Young
The Whispered Kiss
The Windswept Flame
With a Dreamboat in a Hammock

www.ingramcontent.com/pod-product-compliance
Lightning Source LLC
Chambersburg PA
CBHW060044150626
46556CB00018BA/2694